FROM FAR AWAY

It is unusual to see a visitor in the fells in the depths of winter. 'What would bring Leonie Elwood, society beauty and adored child of a millionaire, to the desolate moors on such a day?' wonders the old woman who opens the door and gives her sanctuary, though her heart warns her of the consequences. For Leonie soon loses her heart to Martin Langley, whose mother protects him with the ferocity of a tigress . . .

DOROTHY BLACK

FROM FAR AWAY

Complete and Unabridged

LINFORD
Leicester

First published in Great Britain in 1974 by
Robert Hale And Company
London

First Linford Edition
published 2014
by arrangement with
Robert Hale Limited
London

A catalogue record for this book is available
from the British Library.

ISBN 978–1–4448–1898–7

Published by
F. A. Thorpe (Publishing)
Anstey, Leicestershire

Set by Words & Graphics Ltd.
Anstey, Leicestershire
Printed and bound in Great Britain by
T. J. International Ltd., Padstow, Cornwall

This book is printed on acid-free paper

1

The military car appeared suddenly on the road below the great shoulder of the fells. All around, as far as the eye could reach, winter hills swept away below winter sky. The hills waited, locked in that brooding stillness which any dweller in the Cumberland fells would recognise for the warning of snow to come.

The girl at the wheel of the Jaguar sports was a townswoman born and bred. She might not be able to read the weather . . . but she could feel the countryside. It's like getting onto the roof of the world Leonie Elwood thought. It was frightening — or perhaps awe-inspiring came nearer the truth.

. . . The Jaguar slowed, gave a warning cough, and came to a stop.

And in the same moment, the first

snowflakes glanced athwart the windscreen . . .

Of all places, of all times, to find oneself out of petrol! A countryside without a sign of human life, and a snowfall just beginning.

She got out of the car, examined the tank to make sure of the worst, and stood thinking. Something barely registered as the time slid back into her mind; yes — there had been a thread of smoke going up straight into the still air, a glimpse of grey walls, of deep roofs, and of outbuildings flanking a yard behind a solid stone wall.

How far back? A mile? More, perhaps. She locked the car and set off up the road.

The snow was thickening, slanting in a white curtain. The girl lowered her head and walked fast, feeling the silk scarf knotted under her chin become soaked and chill and the snow trickle inside the collar of her coat. She scarcely heeded it.

It is unusual to see a visitor to the

2

fells in the depths of winter. And such a figure as that of the girl now battling her way through the thickening snow to Felstead Farm. Her soaked scarf was of heavy silk, an exquisite design in pale pink peonies and silvery leaves, bearing the signature of a renowned fashion house. Her coat was of heavy suede lined with lambskin soft and white as the flying snowflakes. It was impossible to see anything of the wearer at the moment, but she was slender, agile, and very graceful, even in a buffeting snowstorm. She went through the snow like a young deer.

What would bring Leonie Elwood, twenty-one-year-old 'Society beauty', adored only child of Albert Elwood, machine-tool millionaire — (or would be, but for taxes . . .) to the waste lands and desolate moors of the north on a bitter winter day?

It was the events leading up to this winter day which raced before Leonie's eyes and made her all but impervious to the growing menace of the weather . . .

Albert Elwood and his wife, Gladys, would give their child the sun, moon and stars, if it could be done.

The Elwood couple had, in their own private, never-uttered phrase, 'come up the hard way', and they had come far and come high up indeed. It was a far cry from the days of the council house and then the suburban semi-detached, to these, when the great lorries and vans rolled about England with the single name ELWOOD to denote some of the best machine tools in the world.

They lost a baby in the early years of their married life. By the time that Leonie came, ten long years later, the Elwood money was rolling in and Gladys Elwood had learned ambition, snobbery, and some other totally false values. Both parents concentrated fanatically on the only child. And as Leonie grew into a beautiful girl, the ambition and snobbery soared, on her behalf, to fantastic heights.

'With those looks — and the money — she can marry where she chooses,' said Gladys Elwood to her husband.

Leonie went to an exclusive and expensive school, Leonie went to Paris for a year, to a select 'finishing establishment' run by a French *comtesse*. And came home to make her social début in London and to be one of the beauties of the year, and in her mother's words, to make a suitable match.

Alaric Brooke was undoubtedly a candidate. He was one of the most eligible young men in London. Not much money, perhaps, but he would come into the ancient family title before very long. Young Alaric Brooke's wife could look ahead to finding herself Lady Brooke of Chenworthy . . .

And where could you see a more attractive couple? Leonie was tall (but not too tall —) slender, rounded, and her lovely face held something of the soft but firm contours of a child's face. Long, night-black hair was parted above her low white forehead and knotted on her neck.

Leonie's eyes were that rare grey-hazel which changes as certain precious stones do, under light or against colours.

Her father once remarked: 'I'll be darned if I know what girls want, nowadays. There's the Milvery girl working in a travel bureau, and photographs of Lord Athelstone's twin daughters in their riding stables. It seems the idea is, get a job and you won't be bored. None of them *need* to earn their bread-and-butter, that's the point.

'Well — no nonsense of that sort about Leo, thank heaven. She knows when she's well-off. She enjoys it all.'

'I should hope so!' her mother said.

Leonie certainly and thoroughly enjoyed what money — her father's money — could buy. Or rather, she took it for granted. She had been surrounded with comfort from her cradle and with increasing luxury and beauty since she was old enough to notice surroundings at all. And yet, there was about her a certain springtide freshness, a simplicity which had grace, not awkwardness.

But neither Mr. and Mrs. Elwood nor anyone else in their London world realised that the girl, with her enjoyment of life and her attractive, spontaneous and natural ways, was groping, inwardly uncertain and baffled, for something which she had not yet found . . .

To the Elwoods, young Alaric Brooke was not only the answer to The Maiden's Prayer but the answer to any Parent's Petition. A very pleasant, eminently presentable young man, rather quiet than otherwise. Which was all to the good.

But the days are past when a girl could be compelled into marrying any man though there are less obvious ways of bringing about a marriage.

'See here, Leo-cub,' her father said, using the pet-name of nursery days, 'you'll be twenty-one in October, and you've refused every chap who's asked

7

you, for nearly three years. Here's young Brooke — everything in his favour, not a thing to be said against him, and you've favoured him more than anyone else ... What are you waiting for? You like him, don't you?'

'Very, very much, Dad. But somehow — not enough, I think. I'm not *sure* — '

Albert Elwood shrugged his massive shoulders.

Gladys spoke to her too ... fondly, indulgently, practically.

'Girls aren't all alike, dearest, by any means. Some fall headlong in love — and look at the results. You've been a bridesmaid half-a-dozen times over, and how many of those romantic love-matches are standing the test?

'The most satisfactory marriages are built on other things, Leo ... And you're not the type ever to fall madly in love ... not till you're actually married, anyway. You're very fond of Alaric; and he's devoted to you. You belong to the same world — '

There was more of this. Much more.

The only item in the repeated recital which held any conviction for Leonie was the assertion: *You're not the type ever to fall madly in love . . . not till you're actually married, anyway . . .* The rest she scarcely heard.

But — she *had* never fallen in love. And she *did* like Alaric more than any other man whom she knew. Maybe it was enough? . . .

The engagement was announced with loud fanfare. Announcements in every possible paper, photographs and paragraphs in all the 'glossies', celebration parties.

The strange thing was, that, the higher the tide of these exciting events rose, the more brilliant grew the prospect ahead, the more uneasy Leonie felt . . . In bewilderment and desperation, she tried to confide in her mother.

'Mummie, I can't help it! Alaric's a man heaps of girls would be glad to marry — but I can't feel he's the man for me . . . '

'Darling, of *course* you feel like that

just now! Every girl has an attack of nerves just before the day — '

'But we're not in the Victorian days now!' Leonie broke out with one of her rare explosions of feeling.

'Don't worry, love! You'll laugh at yourself, a week from now!'

A week from now. That was the date of the wedding.

And this conversation between the mother and daughter had taken place exactly five days ago.

Then — why was Leonie Madeleine, only daughter of Mr. and Mrs. Albert Elwood, driving over the Cumberland fells two days before her much-publicised wedding day? . . .

* * *

Half-an-hour earlier as the sky had sunk over the fells, Martin Langley paused as he crossed the great yard of Felstead Farm and looked up at the grey depths which almost seemed to be resting on the wide old chimneys and deep roofs.

This drawing-near of the sky on the hills is a feature of the north country atmosphere. Suddenly, the peaks take a step forward like ranks of giants closing in on you . . . It is merely a matter of weather; but it is uncanny.

'Snow,' he said briefly with an upward jerk of his head. 'The sheep must be brought in before it breaks.'

Robert Langley nodded and went through the gate. He was the older by four years, a man of thirty, but it was significant that he accepted his younger brother's suggestion, uttered in Martin's extraordinarily quiet, measured tones.

Robert was a tall man but spare, slight in build and his dark, alert face was somehow not the face of a countryman at all. Sensitive, keenly intelligent, and expressive; with some underlying unrest and dissatisfaction lying in the keen dark eyes.

Martin Langley towered, a fair-headed giant of a man, and his fine, sculptured face and sea-blue eyes were as much a contrast to his brother's in spirit as in feature and colouring. Imperturbable calm sealed that face.

Robert, the eldest son, was farming Felstead as his ancestors had done, because his widowed mother took for granted that he would do that and nothing else. But his deepest interest and his talent lay in anything mechanical. He had acquiesced in a fate that set him in a farm which gave next to no scope for mechanisation. He belonged to today and the tempo at which life is lived today. He was shackled to a shared inheritance which belonged to yesterday.

For Martin, sheep-farming was the life of his choice And the fell country-side his natural setting. He had teeming ideas for modernising Felstead, branching out, etc., and unlike Robert, was in perpetual battle and argument with their mother on the subject.

Martin came into the huge kitchen where two women were at work.

Georgina, the woman who worked

for the Langleys, was a lean, silent figure, peeling and slicing vegetables at a sink at the far end of the room. Janet Langley, the mother, the matriarch, and the mistress of Felstead, turned as her son came in.

She was not a big woman. She had no ample imposing presence. Which made it all the more remarkable that she could maintain an iron rule in a home which held grown sons, a son's young wife and grandchildren. She was small, compared with her menfolk. A little, wiry woman, whose sharp face was high-coloured with snapping, light grey eyes and a thin, tight-lipped mouth. Her dark hair piled in plaits on top of her head was barely threaded with grey.

'What brings you indoors at this time of day?' she asked.

Martin pointed to the deep-set windows.

'We're in for a big snow. Rob and Jim and I are going after the sheep.'

'It may be a long business. You'll be

wanting some sandwiches — '

Georgina half-turned from the sink, wiping her hands on her rough apron.

'Coomin' down thick a'ready,' she said briefly. 'Will tha take some o' the cold beef and the cheese? Ye'll be fair clemmed afore ye all get back.'

'Leave it be, Gina, I'll see to it myself,' Janet Langley ordered.

Meanwhile, Robert, having summoned the man, Jim, went up the front staircase to the room where his wife, Ruth lay in the mammoth old four-poster with her week-old baby in a warm basket on the chair beside her.

'How're you feeling, lass?' he asked tenderly.

'Fine,' she answered, smiling up at him. Ruth felt her strength returning with every day; she was up here in peace and quiet, away from the busy doings of the house, away from the clatter and clamour of the two older children, Robby, aged six, Janey, aged four. Away, above all, from the domineering and the harrying of her

14

husband's formidable mother . . .

'Having a baby's a demoralising thing! I've got so lazy that I feel I'd like to stay up here for weeks and weeks — '

Robert's forehead knitted with worried tension. He knew well enough what lay behind the half-joking words. Ruth put a hand quickly on his.

'I didn't mean it, Rob. I was only making a silly joke.'

'I wish more than that,' he said in a fervent tone. 'I wish to heaven we were away, on our own, together, Ruthie. You, and me, and the children. I wish it more than ever, since *he* came — ' he half-rose, bent over the basket where his newborn son lay.

'Be fair, dear! She — your mother — has looked after me well, and better than well, through this time. And she's very, very fond of Rob and Janey.'

'It's not every woman would wish to have her sons and her son's wife and children under her — thumb,' Robert countered with controlled bitterness. 'Well, I must be away, Ruthie. 'It's starting to snow, and hard, by the look of it, and we must get the sheep in.'

Ruth lay thinking of all that was implied, contained, in the few words which had just passed between them.

She was a gay, high-spirited girl when Robert brought her to Felstead as a bride. It had seemed rather a wonderful arrangement, this shared family life in the roomy old house. How quickly that dream had gone to pieces! And what a different reality took its place!

She found in Janet Langley a woman who ruled her household, her affairs, and their affairs with a rod of iron. She found that there was only peace in that house at one price: submission. At first Ruth had argued and protested on her own account, and she would still fight, fiercely and protectively, where her children were concerned. But she had learned to give way on most other counts, for the sake of peace. And because it was unbearable to see her Rob, whom she adored, torn between the two of them, his mother and his wife.

Lying here in the firelight and shadows, Ruth reminded herself of other things, incongruous inexplicable things, which sometimes tilted the balance in the other direction and left you baffled and wondering. Janet Langley could argue with herself, the children's mother; but she never said a harsh word to the children. They knew no fear of Gran ... Ruth had seen sudden tenderness in her sharp, shrewd eyes as she watched small Janey darting through the house like a bird.

Janet had nursed and tendered her through the birth of three children and with the utmost care, if without any trace of feeling ...

Janet, left a young widow, had worked the family farm, conducted the business, invested the profits. Everything she did through those years of labour and loneliness was done for her children. Never for herself. She never went on a holiday. No new clothes for her, until she needed them beyond question. No jaunts to Blackpool or Scarborough — or London. Felstead took every waking hour of her time, and many when she should have been asleep . . .

Ruth was not introspective, but her whole mind was keyed up to a higher and tighter pitch than usual and her imagination more alive. She lay pondering, for the first time; what had turned Janet Langley into the woman which she was?

Other women, ran Ruth's thoughts, have been left young widows with children; and it hasn't made them hard and tyrannical . . . And Rob's mother didn't have poverty to cope with. In her own way, she cares deeply for her children — especially Martin and Barbara . . . I think she's always aggravated with Rob, partly because she knows his heart is not in the farming, and partly — well, because he doesn't stand up to her more . . . my poor love!

She's set all her hopes and aims on Martin, and she's secretly very, very proud of him, but she couldn't show it, to save her life, and they oppose one another at every turn.

. . . I never was able to make out just what she felt about Barbie. Barbie is so lovely . . . so unlike her mother . . . Mrs. Langley always treated her as she treated nobody else . . . It was almost as though she could hardly believe Barbara belonged to her in flesh and blood.

Yet, for all this, thought Ruth, Barbara walks out of her home, at nineteen, and it is her mother who is responsible . . .

I don't know — and I don't think anyone else does — whether that romance of Barbara's and Paul Damer's was the real thing or whether he was the rotter Mrs. Langley made him out to be. All I do know, is, that Barbie was madly *in* love with him. And that, when her mother managed to break it all up, Barbie rushed away to London and got herself a job . . .

The scenes of that short, fleeting

summer sped across the shadows and the flickering firelight. Barbara tapping, light as a mouse, at the thick oak door of the bedroom, whispering, 'Ruthie — Ruthie, are you awake? Come down, will you?'

She would slip from the big bed without waking Robert, and find the girl standing in her dressing-gown, her gold head an aureole in the light of the candle which she held. Barbara would catch Ruth's fingers and rush her down the built-in back stairs to the kitchen. And there they would raid the larder that was like a stone cavern, and sit on the edge of the big kitchen table nibbling ginger parkin and homebaked biscuits and drinking glasses of milk, while Barbara talked . . .

' . . . I saw him today. I walked to the crossroads at Renthwaite, and we drove down to Heronwater and had tea . . . '

Or would it be: ' . . . I caught the bus into Carlisle and he met me there and took me to the pictures.'

Very soon the heady, effervescent outpourings took a different note. Barbara was no longer a young girl, giddy and excited over a first love-affair. She was a girl in love.

' . . . Oh Ruthie, I never knew I could feel like this. It's such heaven that it *hurts*.'

'Barbie — ' Ruth interrupted the flow of ecstasy, 'have you stopped to think what your mother will say when she finds out about this?'

Barbara interrupted in turn. Her eyes blazing, her cheeks on fire.

'He's coming to see Mother tomorrow! So there! She should be pleased and proud that he wants to marry me. He could marry a dozen girls in his own London world — but it's me he loves and wants to marry.'

'Oh, don't talk rubbish!' Ruth broke out impatiently. You could marry any man for miles round, and you know it.'

Barbara laughed, her anger vanishing, and gave her brother's wife a quick kiss.

'Let's not have words, you and I! You've been the only one I could turn to, all through, and I'll never forget it. Tomorrow will be pretty awful, I know — I shall be thankful when it's over. But there simply isn't a thing even Mother could object to, about my marrying Paul . . . '

Ruth shivered involuntarily before the girl's blind confidence.

. . . The radiant delusion was quickly and harshly dispelled. No one except Mrs. Langley and Paul Damer would ever know exactly, down to last word, what took place.

'Darling, leave me to handle this,' he said with a kiss. 'I know enough about your mother to know that it's not going to be any bed of roses, this interview . . . it will be easier for me if you are not there.'

He met Janet Langley's unyielding gaze with a disarming smile, and these words:

'You don't know me, Mrs. Langley; my name is Damer.'

He got no further. Janet said in a tone of steel:

'I know a fair deal about you, Mr. Damer. News travels in these parts faster than in towns . . . and I know you've been hanging about my girl. And I've made it my business to make enquiries about you . . . '

The ordeal was not a lengthy one. Janet Langley went to the point when she said bluntly:

'My daughter's nineteen, as no doubt you know. Till she's twenty-one I can forbid you ever to come inside my doors again, and I do. When she's of age, I can't stop her from marrying any ne'er-do-well she's crazy enough to choose. But let me tell you one thing, Mr. Damer: she'll never see a penny of the Felstead money if she marries you.'

That settled the matter, as far as Paul Damer was concerned. He had indeed lost his shrewd head, and his heart (such as it was) to the golden girl whom he found in the depths of the remote fells. But he had learned that there was money ahead for Barbara . . . and that had drawn him to decide on marriage. Now he knew from her mother's bitter lips he would not be marrying the girl who was heiress to one-third of the Felstead farm but a girl who was penniless.

Barbara sprang from the oak settle in the farmhouse entrance as the parlour door swung open and slammed shut, and Paul Damer, his face white and set, strode to the front door. She caught his arm.

'Paul — Paul — what has happened?'

He stopped, breathing hard, looking down at her, on his face a queer mingling of expressions. Frustration and anger: shame: and longing.

'Your mother has ordered me off the place,' he got out hoarsely.

Barbara gave a cry.

'Why? Why? What did she say?'

'What does it matter what she said? It's all lies . . . ' Paul returned hurriedly. 'She means to choose whom you marry,

24

Barbara — that she made absolutely clear. I think she's not quite sane — I do indeed.

'Anyway — there's no place for me here. I'll write to you, sweet,' he promised rapidly, in the same breathless way. 'I'll write to you, never fear. I — we — shall get nowhere by making any more scenes with your mother. Just wait till you hear from me.'

He caught her roughly in his arms, kissed her as he had never kissed her yet. And was gone.

There followed the two strangest days which had ever ticked themselves away, hour by hour, within the solid old walls of Felstead. Not a word was exchanged between a white-faced Barbara and her mother, whose face had assumed a mask of stone. Ruth waited in an anguish of dread for the storm to break.

Two days of silence and foreboding. On the third, Barbara vanished ... leaving a note which said, '*I am going away. I shall get myself a job. You have driven me to this. You need not imagine that I am going to Paul, nor send either of the boys after me, Mother. I am going to make my own life in my own way because you have made it unbearable for me at home.'*

It was not a Victorian melodrama. It was the 1970s, not the 1870s. When Martin arrived home to be met by the story, a telegram had just arrived from Barbara:

'Have got job waitress in café stop room in Y.M.C.A. stop Don't worry. Barbara.'

It was addressed, not to her mother, but to Martin.

And that, perhaps, was the sharpest and bitterest pang of all for Janet Langley . . .

'It's all so *ordinary* . . . ' Ruth burst out one night to Robert. 'It's just as if Barbie had merely gone off to London to work as thousands of girls do. No one but ourselves would ever guess that your mother and she have just about

26

broken each other's hearts . . . '

For that was what it amounted to. Janet Langley was sick at heart and desolate in inward loneliness, knowing that she had lost her girl. And knowing that it was her own doing.

The secret of what had made Janet into the hard, embittered creature which she was, was unguessed by any of her children. Barbara alone of the three might have realised that something still terribly vulnerable, uncomforted, and hungering, lay buried deep below that unassailable surface but she was too young, too hurt, too angered, to see anything but what her mother had done to her.

She wrote home quite often, and one of her unrevealing, conversational letters had come this very morning. And had left her mother upset, unreasonably disappointed, and sore in heart, for the day.

The long, grey day moved on . . .

★ ★ ★

Robert had just completed the long day's herding. The flocks were safely penned. He came down the steep road to the front of the house and stopped at the sight of the girl who stood on the doorstep in the blinding snow.

'Can I help you?' he asked kindly and courteously.

'Yes, please, if you will! I've run out of petrol about a mile down the road.'

'Where are you bound for?' Robert asked. 'If it's far you'd be unwise to go on. We're in for one of the real winter snowfalls — '

'I — I — well, I thought perhaps I could make Carlisle — or some-where — '

'Well, you certainly cannot go on alone,' he said firmly. 'I reckon you don't know the weather up here. It would be dangerous.'

'You are very kind,' Leonie said with desperation shaking her voice, 'but I must go on. I must!'

'What's all this, Rob?'

His mother appeared in the door.

She interrupted Robert's explanation and Leonie's repeated protests in curt, characteristic fashion.

'Don't be a fool, girl! D'you want to die in a snowdrift . . . Robert, send one of the men to tow her car up here.'

She turned to Leonie again.

'You can stay at Felstead till the storm's over — might be a day or two, might be longer. You never can tell at this time of year. We live rough,' she added with a pride which, once again, belied her words, 'but you're welcome to what we have.'

She led the way to the great kitchen, warm, lamp-lit, the vast table spread for an ample high tea, the windows black panes against the dense whiteness of the falling snow.

Janet disappeared into the upper regions, and Leonie stood before the roaring range, shuddering in the sudden onslaught of heat.

The silence was broken by a sound of running water and splashing from the scullery, and the jerk of a roller-towel.

Martin Langley came into the room.

They stood facing one another. The fair-headed Viking of a man, his fine face and stalwart frame showing marks of evident weariness. The girl in a wool dress the blue of periwinkles in a hedge, which made her lovely eyes look blue in the firelight, her rounded face whipped to rose-flame by the snow and clear of make-up as a child's face.

Leonie smiled faintly, uncertainly. But Martin's face was full of sudden astonishment. And of recognition . . .

'Good evening, Miss Elwood,' he said. 'It is Miss Elwood, isn't it? Miss — Leonie Elwood?'

She gasped.

'How — did you know?'

Martin smiled.

'Even farm folk read the papers . . . Your photograph, and the piece about your wedding next week were in the *Morning News* — and nearly full-page in the *Daily Post* . . . '

Leonie would never know what impelled her to speak the truth to this utter stranger and in the first moments of meeting. She was not to recognise the moment for what it was: a moment which *was* truth . . . a meeting between two human beings who, even before they know it, see one another 'not in a glass darkly, but . . . face to face . . . '

It is an experience rare enough, in all conscience.

'You're wondering — why I'm here at all. Yes, yes,' as Martin made a movement of his head, 'of course you are. *And — I want to tell you* . . . I don't know why,' she said, almost wildly.

She poured out the broken sentences, briefly enough. And Martin stood where he was, his eyes fixed on her working, quivering face, without inter-rupting the incoherent story.

Leonie's voice died away on the final words.

'I had to come away — I couldn't help myself — something *drove* me . . . '

Then, Martin's deep, measured voice said slowly,

31

'Maybe something led you, Miss Elwood ... You might have gone anywhere — but you land here, and Felstead'll be snow-bound for days at least, I can tell you that much. You'll have time to think, here, among strangers, and you may be sure no one here will ask questions of you. Stay as long — or as little — as you need. By the time the snow lets up, you'll know whether your mind's set to go on — or go back.'

The slow, deliberate words fell on her ears in the firelight and shadows like the slow sound of bells or the deep notes of an organ.

A voice in Martin Langley's brain was saying, 'You never loved him. You, being you, would never have run away if you had. God send you never change your mind ... you cannot go back. You must not ...'

Into the palpitating silence, alive with portent, vibrant with blind forces felt but not yet understood, came Janet's harsh voice: 'Well, lad? So you're back.

Martin this is Miss — ?'

Leonie said with an effort, 'my name is Elwood — Leonie Elwood. Your son — recognised me from the newspapers — '

'Elwood, is it? I know *that* name . . . ' Janet gave a dry laugh. 'Are you kin to the Machine-Tools King, as I've heard him called?'

'I am his daughter,' Leonie said.

'Since you've been given shelter here,' she said bluntly, 'I reckon I've the right to ask this much: Why are you journeying in this neighbourhood in dead winter, so far from your home? I hope you're not running from the police . . . ?'

Martin uttered a sharp, wordless sound, and took a step forward.

But Leonie laughed, a quivering, breathless laugh.

'Not the police this time, Mrs. Langley. Only my own wedding — ' she answered.

And burst into tears . . .

2

Martin was swept by a surge of such feelings as he had never known: anger at his mother's blunt harshness and a sense of unbearable pity at the sight of the sudden tears stealing down a girl's face.

Martin was the only one of the Langleys who knew no fear of his mother, and consequently never felt the baffled anger which you only feel against someone whom you are not strong enough to resist, and you know it. He was used to her hard ways.

So, why, in the name of reason, should he find himself trembling through all his great frame with mingled revolt and compassion?

Before he could clear his head, Martin received another shock. Of surprise, this time. He heard his mother say with a sort of gruff gentleness,

'Well, well, that's your own affair, then. And I'll not be prying into it. Come upstairs, now. and see your room and find your way about the house.'

At this point, Janey and Rob clattered down the steep back stairs and tumbled into the room.

'Gran — Gran — what do you think? We've bin seein' the new baby in his *bath* — '

Leonie looked enquiringly from one small, excited face to the other, and then at Mrs. Langley.

'These are my grandchildren,' Janet said. 'And the new one — a boy — is upstairs.'

'A new baby? Then — oh dear! this is an awful time for a stranger to come down on you!' Leonie exclaimed uneasily.

'And why? There's room and to spare in this house for many more than's in it,' Janet returned.

She spoke to the children:

'This lady is Miss Elwood. Janey, Rob, take her upstairs to the Oak

Room, that's where she is going to sleep. And show her the bathroom and the way down by the front stairs.'

'Come along,' Janey invited her, and each slipped a hand into one of Leonie's. Together they climbed the steep, dark staircase. It rose to a long L-shaped passage, wide as an average-sized room, one wall set with heavy old doors, the other with heavy oak cupboards or presses. At the far end of the shorter wing a door stood open and Rob said solemnly,

'There's a step down — '

Leonie gave a small gasp. She stood in a huge, low room whose floor sloped unevenly and whose windows were set high in the thick wall, small latticed windows above a wide sill. The room held an assortment of heavy, old furniture. A colossal wardrobe, a splendid fourposter bed stripped of its curtains, two tall chests of drawers, odd tables and chairs. The newly-lit fire blazed and crackled hearteningly in a big fireplace.

'What a beautiful room!' Leonie said. 'And what's that door in the corner?'

With a shout of glee, the children tugged it open. A tiny chamber or closet, with yet another small, high-set window and a cavity in the wall like a shelf cut into it.

'It's a *powder*-room,' Janey proclaimed.

As Leonie stood, still shivering in the firelight a sense rose about her and stole through her, of the ancient heritage of dignity and solid pride which was a part of Felstead . . .

Life here might be stark in its simplicity and hard toil and its solitude. But there was something as enduring as time itself in such a house . . . and she knew without yet being told, that the family who now lived under its warren of mellow roofs and chimney-stacks was the same family which had lived here for generations past . . .

'Gran said to show her the bath-room,' Rob prompted.

'It's ever so far away,' Janey said with

relish. 'You better hold my hand — '

Leonie was conducted into the largest bathroom she had ever seen. The fittings were about as old-fashioned as they could well be, including a bath-tub designed for giants and encased in mahogany . . . but Leonie could at least wash her numbed hands in a flow of steaming hot water and wince as they tingled and stung.

'Would you like to see Mummie and the baby?' Janey proposed jubilantly.

'Very much. But I think I had better wait to ask your Grannie.'

'Well, come downstairs then,' Janey said, taking her role of guide with blissful importance.

They went down the wide, beautiful staircase where an arched window rose to the ceiling.

'Oo — *look* at the snow!' Rob said. They stood to look through the black panes where the steady, inexorable fall of white flakes had something actually menacing to Leonie's eyes.

Leonie was anything but a fragile

plant. She had enjoyed winter holidays in Switzerland. She had once spent Christmas with a schoolfriend of Paris days in a family *château* among wild pine forests. But something incomprehensible and indefinable crept through her as she watched the snow from the staircase window. This living wall of snow, ruthlessly enclosing her and the household of strangers, held some power.

Then the children, jumping down the last steps and chattering, broke the uneasy spell.

'Come an' see the parlour — '

'Why? We don't, ever — an' it'll be cold!'

'Gran said *show* her things — '

So Leonie was shown another great room, cold as an ice-box, indeed, and crowded with old-fashioned furniture and nick-nacks. She was shown a dining-room with twelve black oak chairs ranged up and down a table where nearly double the number of persons could be seated, a sideboard about as big as a family coach loaded with silver which gleamed in the twilight.

'Those cups and things are what Daddy and Uncle Martin win bercoz of the sheep,' Rob remarked lucidly.

They came back to the kitchen at last. The household was sitting down to tea. The room was a core of light and glowing warmth after the frozen and shadowy stillness of the rambling old house. The two men got to their feet, and Martin pulled out a chair for Leonie.

Leonie felt a baffling contrast between the surroundings and the meal and the atmosphere. Here was the vast kitchen, glowing with warmth from the range, the hanging light above the table shedding a clear circle of light on to the white cloth and the lavish spread of home-made scones and rich dark parkin (the famous spiced gingerbread of the north), the platter of ham, the array of eggs under knitted cosies. Firelight and shadows played on the dresser of black

40

polished oak which rose to the high ceiling. The chairs ranged at the long table were oak-backed with rush-seats.

It was a picture of homeliness and the dignity that belongs to homely things at their best.

But it was (to Leonie), an uneasy meal . . .

The two men sat and ate and drank in almost total silence. Leonie did not know that the man who has passed a heavy working day in the open air is seldom talkative at the end of such days.

So, here sat Leonie, and across the expanse of the table, opposite to her, she saw the fair-haired Viking, Martin Langley, who, less than an hour ago, had appeared to her out of the blue, a stranger who, by some indescribable and incomprehensible miracle, was no stranger. To whom she had suddenly opened her troubled heart, and who had answered her, in his slow, deep voice of immense quietude and power, with complete understanding.

Now he had, it seemed, retreated across a divide wider by far than the loaded table. His clear eyes met hers without expression.

It was an evening so packed and overloaded with new impressions for the girl, that she could not sort them out nor even dwell upon them. That would come later.

Later on, when Leonie would learn more, with every day, of the household into which she had come, she was to recognise, dimly, that some deep wisdom, some commonsense, and affection, must have gone to the training of two children as happy and as untroublesome as these. And that the credit was due in great measure to the small, powerful woman who sat at the head of the table and wielded the great teapot as she wielded every other concern of her household's teeming existence . . .

It was Robert Langley, the spare, dark man with the oddly sensitive face and shadowed eyes, who seemed uncertain and ill-at-ease with his mother. Robert smiled, a swift, apologetic smile, when Janet Langley happened to speak to him. Even if it were only to direct him.

'Pass me Miss Elwood's cup, Robert. Wake up, lad!'

I do believe he's afraid of his mother — even if his children aren't . . . Leonie thought.

Janet Langley made what might be described as hostess conversation.

'It's a real pity you should come to these parts in this weather, Miss Elwood. Visitors to Cumberland think it a rare bit of country. Folk like ourselves that live in it all the year round take it for granted, I daresay.'

'Oh, I know how wonderful Cumberland must be!' Leonie answered eagerly. 'I have an aunt who lives in Carlisle and whenever she comes south she can't stop talking about it.'

'As a matter of fact — ' the colour rose in Leonie's face — 'I rather thought I'd go to her . . . And then, I

43

realised — I remembered — that she's away just now — '

It sounded lame enough, and trivial enough. But there was sudden understanding in Martin's eyes. He grasped what lay beneath the faltered words. Aunt Whatever-her-name-might-be, was, of course, on her way to the wedding from which the bride was running for dear life.

A touch of amusement, rigidly suppressed, was on Martin's lips. His mother had thawed in manner as Leonie spoke. An aunt in Carlisle carried more weight with Janet Langley than the fact that the name Elwood was on hoardings all over the country.

When the meal came to an end, Leonie looked appealingly at her hostess.

'Mrs. Langley — please — you will let me help with all this washing-up?'

Janet said, mildly enough but decidedly, 'That's kind of you, Miss Elwood. But it would only put Georgina out — to have a stranger getting in her way . . . '

Leonie flushed, Martin stiffened slightly as he went to the door.

'Then — perhaps I could help to put Janey and — Robin, is it? — to bed? Give them their baths?'

'We have our baths in the morning, till Mum can get up again and help us at bedtime,' Janey said.

'Couldjoo tell us some stories?' Rob proposed suddenly, gazing at Leonie with pleased confidence.

'I — I expect so,' Leonie answered.

Janet gave a brisk shrug of her thin shoulders but the half-smile on her face was indulgent.

'They're full of fancies, those two. What with their Uncle Martin bringing them those 'comics' every time he has to go to the post office . . . and their mother telling them all manner of old tales about the countryside hereabouts . . . If it isn't space-men and rockets to the moon, it's stories about Roman soldiers here in Cumberland and dear knows what.'

On a table at the foot of the kitchen

stairs stood a row of candles in flat candlesticks. And on a bracket beside the front stairs, a small electric lantern. Although there was electric light at Felstead, the corridors were unlit.

Leonie carried a lighted candle as she went down the long passage with the children on either side of her. A door at the end stood ajar and lamplight stole softly into the gloom and the shadows. A sweet voice called, 'Janey — Robbie — are you there?'

'Mummie's awake!' Rob said happily. And Janey tugged at Leonie's hand, 'Come in and see the new baby! You *can* — Mummie's awake, and he hardly ever is . . .'

Leonie stood hesitating in the door.

Thus it was that Ruth, raising herself on her elbow in the great bed, had her first sight of the stranger. A slender, motionless figure framed in the black oak doorway, a candle in one hand, the wavering, pointed light rising beneath a lovely oval face, dark hair gleaming in wings from the white

46

parting, star-clear eyes, and beautiful, shyly-smiling mouth.

Ruth caught a breath. Put out a hand. And said, '*Come in, Bride* . . . '

Leonie gasped. Had the news reached this remote, enfolded room already, where a young woman lay apart from the household hustle and voices with her newborn child?

Ruth smiled.

'I'm sorry! That slipped out! You don't know our Cumberland legend of Saint Bride, then?'

Leonie shook her head, mystified.

'She was a little handmaid to the Mother of Jesus,' Ruth said softly. 'She walked before the donkey which carried the Mother and Child, bearing a candle to light the road . . . Here, in parts of Cumberland, as a new baby is born, the midwife sometimes says '*Come in, Bride* . . . ' it's a sort of blessing, really . . .

'As you stood there with that candle — the words came into my head. That's all!'

Leonie swallowed. There was a lump in her throat.

'I see. It's — a sweet legend . . . I never heard it before. May I look at the baby?'

Ruth nodded, smiling. And Leonie looked at a minute pink face, minute clenched fists, and a thatch of soft, silky down.

'He looks — very big for a new one,' she said uncertainly. 'How new is he?'

'Just a week.'

'What are you calling him?'

'Martin.'

Ruth thought that she saw the newcomer give a slight start. It was as though a tremor ran through the slender, graceful figure beside the basket-cot.

'I feel horribly in the way, you know?' Leonie said, turning back to the bed. 'With you — up here, and a new baby in the house — '

'You needn't! And I shall be downstairs in two or three days. It seems a shame you should be here when we're practically snowed-up, though,' said Ruth, unconsciously echoing her mother-in-law's words. 'This is such a glorious part of the country — '

'Mrs. Langley said — it was your speaking of that legend which reminded me — that you know all about the history and legends and stories connected with it.'

Ruth laughed.

'Cumberland's chockful of history. There are stone circles as mysterious as Stonehenge itself. There are traces and relics of the Stone Age and the Bronze Age. There are Saxon and Norman pieces in lots of the old churches. But it's the Romans who still haunt Cumberland,' said Ruth, her brown eyes lighting up.

She broke off with an apologetic laugh.

'You've set me off! But you see — I was a school-teacher here before I married and came to Felstead. The history of Cumberland has always — well, *got* me!'

'Riding your hobby-horse, Ruth?' a voice spoke from the door. Martin came into the room.

The big room was warm from the glow of the fire and the bed where Ruth lay was enclosed in a pool of shaded lamplight. But for Leonie, all in a moment, a deeper warmth a clearer and brighter light, stole into the room like an incoming tide . . .

The sense of unease and bewilderment fell away from her. As Martin's eyes rested on hers, unsmiling, penetrating to her very heart, Leonie knew that that first encounter had not been an illusion . . . nor an insane impulse. It was the only, the ultimate reality.

Ruth, from her pillows, watched both faces. And it was she, alone of the three, who felt a pang of perturbation. What in the name of reason has happened? . . . is happening? her thoughts raced.

Martin was smiling down at his brother's wife now.

'Chance for you?' he said teasingly.

'Someone to listen while you dig up Ancient Britain and the glories of Cumberland? You don't know what you're in for,' he told Leonie.

'Uncle Mart — she said she'd tell us a story — ' Rob's voice was patiently reproachful.

'I'll go with them — if it's all right?' Leonie said, looking at Ruth.

She felt no exasperation whatever at the interruption. She could not, for her life, have attempted a bedtime story under Martin's eyes and with every nerve in her aware of nothing but his presence.

There was no heat in the children's room, and Leonie shivered.

'Shall we come into my room and have the story by the fire?' she offered.

They skipped along beside her, but she realised that they were impervious to the cold in their own room. A house like Felstead was a revelation to Leonie in more ways than one. She was accustomed to central heating, but there was, in this enormous old house, a sort of lavish discomfort which belonged to the Middle Ages . . . A fire glowed in the kitchen day and night and the room was always a vast cavern of warmth. But even in the room where Ruth lay in bed, the fire, carefully tended, only made a circle of heat about the hearth, the room was too big to be ever wholly warmed.

Ruth laid a hand on Martin's wrist.

'Mart — what's going on? Who *is* she?'

'Didn't Mother say anything to you?'

'She told me a young lady from London had lost her way, or something, at Huggett's Gap, and that she was sheltering here because the snow has started. And that her name was Wellwood — '

'Elwood. Was that all she said?'

Ruth hesitated.

'Well — you know your mother, Mart . . . She wasn't best pleased at having a stranger here when the snow's begun; she said, 'We may have her on our hands for days, very likely. It was a daft notion, to drive north at this time of year.'

'But, my dear — ' Ruth said anxiously, 'that's neither here nor there. The minute you came in — the minute I saw you two look at one another — I knew there was *something* between you . . . Who *is* she? You know her already?'

Martin gave a short laugh that came on a shaken breath.

'You say — something's between us, Ruthie. I reckon you've gone straight to the root of the matter. There's everything between us. Everything — ' he paused, 'that makes two people into one.'

'But — then — when did you ever meet her before? Your mother said she's a Londoner — '

'I met her for the first time when I found her here, soaking wet from walking her way from the Gap.'

'She'd be beautiful even then,' Ruth said under her breath. 'She came into this room with a candle just now —

and I thought of St. Bride, all in a second . . . '

She passed a hand across her forehead in utter bewilderment.

'I still don't understand!'

'I doubt if I understand, myself,' Martin said soberly. 'I think maybe it goes beyond understanding. I only know it's true.'

Ruth sank back on her pillow.

'For heaven's sake, try to explain?' she urged.

Slowly, Martin drew his shabby leather wallet from his coat pocket, opened it, and took out a page from a magazine which he unfolded and laid on the edge of the sheet. It was a reproduction of an exquisite portrait photograph in modern style — the famous photograph, reprinted when the engagement was announced. It showed the seated figure of a girl in a white dress, and a mirror behind her lovely head which repeated the picture in reflection. No jewel, not even a string of pearls, broke the flawless lines of her throat, her slender arms, her taper fingers. On the narrow carved table beneath the mirror a tall white vase of white rhododendrons rose behind the white shoulders and shining dark head. A branch of the dark, glossy leaves and moon-white blossoms lay across her lap and a single cluster was fastened in her hair, lying low against her neck. Leonie's face was a pale oval against dark leaves and pale blossoms, her clear eyes looked from the picture, serious and shining.

It was not only a beautiful study of a very beautiful girl, but something more. The half-wistful, half-eager look in that lovely young face, the look of one who is searching for something still to find . . .

'Someone staying at the Bridge Inn left this magazine behind,' Martin was saying. 'And I picked it up — goodness knows why! and I came on this.

'I don't know what came over me, Ruth, I don't indeed. It wasn't like looking at a picture. I was looking at *her* . . . and she was looking back at me . . . and at no one else . . . I tore it out, and kept it ever since.

'Then — there were newspapers . . . with more pictures, and pieces about her engagement. And when I read those, I felt as if someone had put a bullet into me.'

Martin walked to the hearth and stood looking into the fire.

'There was a lot about her family and the chap she was going to marry. He's heir to some title . . . and one of those infernal papers called him 'London's most eligible bachelor . . . ' whatever that may mean.

' . . . You asked who she is? She's only daughter — only child — to Elwood, of Machine-Tools. Well — all that brought me down to earth with a vengeance. It wasn't — ' again Martin hesitated, painfully striving to express what he himself hardly understood — 'it wasn't that I'd thought about her in that way. She'd been with me — in my mind, in my eyes, in my blood — ever since I saw that picture. But I'd never said to myself, 'That's the girl I'll marry one of these days . . . ' But when I knew she was marrying this chap — I can't say what I mean, Ruth — ' he broke out in a sort of desperation.

'I think I understand,' Ruth said gently. 'Go on, Martin.'

'Then — a matter of hours ago — she walked in here. And for a second, I felt as though something had blinded me . . . stunned me . . . And then, I knew — ' Martin swung round from the fire, 'I tell you, I *knew*, that this was no chance, no accidental happening. It was meant. It was fate.

'I spoke her name before I realised. And that shook her. And when we were alone for a minute, she suddenly poured it all out to me. That she couldn't go through with it . . . and the wedding's supposed to be this very week.

'We looked at one another,' said Martin, drawing a deep breath. 'And God is my witness I never said one word of what I was feeling. But I knew then that we belong to one another. *And she knew it too.* I saw it in her eyes.

'Whatever's to come, whatever lies ahead, nothing can keep us apart, her and me.'

Ruth covered her eyes with the back of one hand in an unconscious gesture that her own small girl might have used.

She murmured, 'Oh — Mart — my dear!' on a frightened sob. 'It's a madness. Think of her people . . . think of — your mother — '

'I know lass. I know. I know it all. But it's as I've said: it's fate.'

When Leonie came from seeing the children into bed, she went down the shadow-filled tunnel of the great passage candle in hand. And at the turn of the passage a figure moved from the shadows and spoke her name. Martin took the candlestick from her suddenly trembling fingers and set it on the deep ledge of a window set above the head of the stairs. In the pale ring of light, they stood with their eyes fixed on each other's face.

Then he was drawing her to him, she was held close against his heart.

'Love — you know what's happened to us,' said Martin's whisper above her head buried in his shoulder.

'Yes — I know,' Leonie breathed. 'I don't understand — but oh Martin — Martin — I know . . . '

She lifted her face to him, and they stood, without more words, his mouth on hers.

Presently voices and footsteps in the hall far below broke the spell. Leonie started, turned.

'I can't go down again — I can't! Oh — Martin — '

'You needn't. You shan't. Get to bed, my blessed lass, and get to sleep . . . We keep early hours here, anyway.'

He caught her hands and crushed them against his lips, and Leonie took the candle and fled into the shadows.

Janet Langley was winding the kitchen clock when Martin came downstairs.

'Well — I'm for bed,' she announced. 'Where's Miss Elwood?'

'She was with Ruth when I looked in a while ago, and she said something about going to her room.'

'It's a daft business, the whole thing!' Janet said with sudden energy. 'I don't like it at all. Girls have got scared and run away from their wedding before now — I've seen more than one, in my time. But this isn't just any girl.'

'What do you mean by that, Mother?'

'Use your wits,' his mother returned sharply. 'She's Elwood's daughter, isn't she? And Elwood's a rich chap. There was something about the wedding in the Sunday paper that Gina and Jim take — *People's Chronicle*. Jim was sorry he couldn't get down to the Sheepshearers' Arms on account of the snow — he was all set to tell folk that Elwood's girl was here at Felstead.

'This'll be in the news, as they say, Martin, you mark my words. And trouble ahead, and plenty of it. And I've no mind to be mixed up in it.'

'She can hardly have left word that she was coming here,' Martin observed with dry coolness, 'considering that she never knew Felstead or we existed. And the telephone wires are down, so she can't make any contacts.'

'That's all very well,' his mother said. 'And she'll be on her way directly the roads are usable, I know that as well as you do. And where she goes or what she does, is no business of ours: I know that, too.

'But I still don't like it. Trouble will come of it, I can feel that in my bones.

' . . . Why had she to come *here*?'

3

Leonie woke. The room was bitterly cold and brimming with grey darkness. She sat up in bed and lit the candle, because the only light-switch was beside the door.

It was twenty-minutes past five. She blew out the light and huddled down again under the blankets, shivering.

Her thoughts swept down upon her, overpowering and terrifying.

She had no qualms about her flight. That was something which she could not have helped doing. It was inevitable. Her only regrets there, were for whatever hurt and affront was dealt to Alaric Brooke and to her parents. She had spent hours of the night before, writing and re-writing letters to them, left to be found after she slipped from the flat before anyone was awake and got her car out of the garage and drove away.

No! What made her lie huddled down in the great bed, shaking, and with her heart thudding wildly, was everything which had happened since she landed here at Felstead . . .

Did it really happen? Was it a dream? Face to face with young Martin Langley, she had given way without a thought to the sudden overpowering compulsion to pour out to him the reason for her flight and her appearance at Felstead. To a total stranger, whose very name she had only just heard.

Well, that was fantastic enough, irrational enough, if you liked? But that was not even the heart of the matter. Other people, under extreme tension, have been known to unload their burdens on to complete strangers.

But she had looked into Martin Langley's splendid face and steadfast eyes, and — something had happened. It was as though, in a flash of some unearthly light, a link were forged between them.

And then, in the shadows and the wavering candlelight and the tunnel-like passage outside this very room she had gone into his arms . . .

Now it was an ice-cold, winter morning. And the radiance and the exaltation and the surety were gone. And Leonie lay quaking, dismayed and utterly bewildered. And afraid . . .

What would Martin expect of her, now? To what had she committed herself? She was here, in a world remote from her own — a stranger among strangers. Desolate, awe-inspiring country. Huge, dark old house, cruelly cold to anyone used to so different an atmosphere. And at its centre like a spider at the centre of a great web, a hard, hostile old woman, who had mistrusted her at sight and was only counting the time till she should be gone.

What would happen, if Mrs. Langley had even an inkling of what had passed between her son and the unwelcome stranger in her house that was her kingdom?

At last Leonie could bear it no longer. She was shivering so much with nervous chill as with physical cold. The picture came to her of the kitchen — empty, silent, and sure to be warm . . . She lit her candle once more, got into dressing-gown and slippers and went down through the sleeping, shadow-thronged house.

The light was on in the kitchen. Someone was standing at the high dresser, taking down some china which rattled in the silence.

Leonie's gasp was a low cry.

Martin turned and stared at the slender figure in a flowing dressing-gown the green of spring willows, her hair falling to her waist in two long braids.

'What is it?' he asked. And then, intently, 'Leonie — don't look so scared! It's only me!'

'I woke up — and it was so cold — and I got thinking . . . About yesterday . . . Oh, Martin — it doesn't feel real. I don't know — what to do . . .'

For a moment which seemed endless, he looked at her steadily. Then he knelt down at the range, raking the ash, pulling out the damper, so that a dull roar and a leaping glow brought the fire to life.

'Don't worry. And don't be afraid. There's nothing for you to be afraid of, nothing in the world.

' . . . What do you take me for, my dear? Do you think for one minute that I'd try to bind you . . . to make any claims . . . because of yesterday?

'I believe in what happened to us, as I believe in my own soul and yours,' said Martin, using such words as he had never spoken in his life.

'I do, too,' she interrupted in a breathless whisper. 'I do, Martin! Only — I don't know what it means — '

The rare flash of tenderness went across his face.

'That is something which we must both wait to find out,' he said gently.

'Meanwhile, you are here in our home and in our care,' he said with a simplicity which had something regal about it. 'And I'll not speak a word nor make a move, to trouble you.

'And now, sit yourself close to the fire and I'll brew us both a cup of tea.'

Leonie thought, incoherently, that here in this homely kitchen, busy with the homely chore of boiling kettle and brown teapot, Martin towered like some knightly figure of legend. Could any man on earth have met her childish panic with a grander tenderness, a deeper understanding, or a spirit of truer greatness? . . .

★   ★   ★

The snow fell. Day after day, night after night. They were walled-in, a citadel, an enclosed world.

To Leonie, it was as though the heavy oak doors had swung shut upon any other world that she had known.

And the strangest thing of all, was that she was at peace as she had never been before . . .

Peace dropped upon her like a cloak, an enfolding garment. She was one of the household, sharing their isolation, sharing their company which made the isolation a thing of no importance.

Janet's dry look gave way to a grudging approval as Leonie made the big beds with Georgina, used broom and duster (no labour-saving gadgets at Felstead . . .) plied an iron, and even succeeded in doing some of the copious washing.

Ruth was up and about again. And Leonie saw that mother-in-law was seeing to it that Ruth did not take on any of the heavy chores as yet.

'Ruth, how many times have I told you *not* to wash out those nappies yourself? Stooping over the tub . . . wringing 'em out . . . we'll have you crawling about with backache, and a lot of use that'll be . . . I'll rinse them out myself when I've got my soup-stock going.'

'Let me, Mrs. Langley,' Leonie said. Her eyes danced, and widened, as she confronted the quelling old woman.

'Even I can hardly go wrong with nappies?' she suggested demurely.

Janet almost smiled. Almost: not quite.

'You'll find it comes hard on the hands,' she countered.

'I've got hand lotion upstairs. And I've used them on harder jobs. When my father gave me my first car, he sent me into the garage to learn running repairs . . . When I had a pony, I had to learn to groom her myself . . . He says if you want to own anything you must know how to service it.'

'He sounds like a sensible man,' was Janet's comment.

One evening at tea she demanded rather than enquired, 'Who made these scones?'

'Leonie did, Gran. Aren't they lovely?' Janey supplied.

'For someone that's never cooked before, you've a light touch, I'll say that much,' Janet pronounced, sampling a second scone.

'But I have cooked before,' Leonie

said meekly. 'When I was at school in Paris, we all had cookery lessons.'

Martin gave no sign that the newcomer in their midst meant anything more to him than a very lovely being to whom no man could be solidly impervious . . . He made no attempt to get a sight of her or a word with her alone.

But his presence, seen or unseen, was somehow a part of the strange peace which enclosed Leonie like the ancient walls of Felstead and the ramparts of the snowy hills beyond them. She was conscious of his presence even when she did not know where he was, in the deeps of the big house or out on the farm.

She was unexpectedly happy with Ruth and the children.

'You know, it's funny to think I've only been here for four days,' Leonie said to Ruth. 'I mean — I feel as though I'd known you and the children for ages. In fact, as though I'd never *not* known you!'

'I'm glad,' Ruth said simply. She added, half-shyly, 'I never knew the children to take to anybody the way they've taken to you — '

The road to the village school was, of course, impassable, and Leonie had offered, tentatively, to give Robbie and Janey some simple lessons.

Leonie was watching the baby being bathed in a small tub before the bedroom fire as the two girls talked.

Leonie said suddenly, 'Ruth — do many families up here live all together, like you do? Is it a north country custom?'

Ruth's lips tightened, and her brows drew together.

'No!' she answered emphatically.

Their eyes met. Ruth gave a brief half-apologetic laugh.

'You may only have been here for four days, Leonie but you can surely see the way things are at Felstead . . . '

While she completed young Martin's toilet for the night, Ruth went on speaking in the rapid, tense way of someone who is releasing what has long been pent-up.

'When Robert talked of his mother living at Felstead, after we would be married, I didn't pay much heed. That's usual enough, even if it isn't always satisfactory . . . My mother lived with my married sister for a while, after my father died. I knew from Robert that Felstead was a big place, plenty of room. I thought I'd find a widowed mother living in her son's home . . . I didn't reckon on finding that we would be living in a house that was his mother's kingdom . . . and where she ruled everyone and everything.'

'Ruth — don't! Don't upset yourself so!'

Ruth laughed, an odd, forlorn sound.

'I suppose I rather — let myself go, Leonie. I'm sorry. I suppose I'm not really quite up to par, yet.'

'I should think not! The baby isn't two weeks old!'

'I could take anything, if it weren't for what she's done to Robert,' Ruth broke out again. 'He doesn't *want* to farm Felstead, and never has. He's wanted to get away, ever since he was a boy.'

'What does he want to do, then?'

'He's a born mechanical engineer,' Ruth said proudly. 'Machinery . . . it's meat and drink to Robert. And he's not a countryman at heart. He'd rather live in cities . . .

'Then, why didn't he, Ruth?'

'My dear,' said Ruth softly, 'some can fight for their own hand, and others can't . . . That man of mine just isn't the fighting kind. And that's all there is to say about it . . .

'I can fight!' she added with a spark in her brown eyes. 'And at first — I did! But it did no good, only made things harder for Robert.

'It was easier — better — once the children came . . . I didn't think it would be, I was worried that she might be harsh and unkind towards a child. But she wasn't! — '

'No! That was one of the very first

things that I noticed. The children don't seem to be in the very least afraid of her — '

'They're not! They're very fond of her, in fact. And I — ' Ruth laughed softly. 'I'm *important*, you see? because of them ... She looks after me thoroughly, when a baby is coming.'

'Does Martin feel the same as Robert — about the farm and the life here?' Leonie asked.

She had no idea that Martin and herself had bared their shaken and bewildered hearts to Ruth's eyes in the first hour of meeting. Nor that Martin had spoken to his sister-in-law as he could have spoken to no one else.

Ruth felt an instant self-consciousness ...

'Oh, no! No! Martin belongs here, body and soul. He *is* Felstead ... He's a fellsman, first and last ... The only tug-of-war between him and his mother is that he's all for getting the farm on to a more modern footing and she's set against it. But he even wins — some-times.'

Leonie gave a little unconscious shiver.

'It's rather — awful, isn't it? The whole situation. I mean. I wonder what makes Mrs. Langley so hard and bitter? She doesn't seem to get much enjoy-ment out of having her own way at every turn.'

'I know other managing older women — ' Leonie was groping her way aloud, 'but they do at least seem to get some — well, *fun* out of it!'

'She's been more warped and unhappy than ever, since that affair of Barbara's . . . but she was never a happy woman, even before that — '

'Barbara? Who is Barbara?'

Ruth looked round in surprise.

'Somehow, I took for granted that you knew about that! The truth is, Leonie — I forget you've only been here for a matter of days! You seem to — be part of the household — '

Leonie said impulsively, 'When I'm

up here with you — or when I'm doing anything with Robbie and Janey — I have that feeling, too. But everything about Mrs. Langley makes me feel as though I'd got into the sort of world you find yourself in when you're having a bad dream! . . . '

She broke off, with an apologetic little laugh.

'That sounds horribly rude and ungrateful, doesn't it? When she's taken me in and given me hospitality, and with circumstances very obviously against me . . .

'I'm beginning to realise what an idiotic thing I did, Ruth, in *bolting* like that! Silly, and cowardly, and selfish — '

Ruth nodded, slowly. She was much too honest to deny it.

'But go on about Barbara — whoever she is,' Leonie prompted her.

Ruth came back to the fire.

'Barbara is the daughter, Leonie, the only daughter — '

'Good heavens! I can't imagine Mrs. Langley with a daughter!' Leonie exclaimed naïvely.

'She's a lovely girl,' Ruth said. 'If you can picture a girl as fair-haired and good-looking as — Martin is, only slight and nothing like so tall — that's Barbie. And Mrs. Langley fairly doted on her . . . though you'll say you can't imagine that either.

'You see, my dear, north country folk don't express their feelings easily — their softer feelings, at any rate. I'll try to explain. In the big parlour — you've seen it, haven't you? — there's a cabinet of china which our vicar, Mr. Shaw, says is fit for a museum.

'It's never used, as you may well suppose. But Mrs. Langley keeps the key of that cabinet, and every so often she takes out those delicate, beautiful cups and saucers, and so forth, and washes them herself.

'The children were in her bedroom one day when she was sorting drawers, and I happened to go in to ask her something. And Janey said. 'Jus' look, Mum — look at Gran's lovely, lovely things!' There was an old leather case open on a table, and in it was one of those old-fashioned, Victorian sets, a heavy, elaborate necklace, and a big brooch, and long, intricate earrings — Whitby jet, and seed-pearls, and all set in gold.

'Mrs. Langley gave that short, gruff laugh of hers, she sounded almost embarrassed. 'Gew-gaws!' she said. I said, 'But they're handsome, Gran! And valuable, too, I should think? Don't you even wear the brooch?' She came back like a pistol-shot: 'Don't talk so daft, girl. I'd look a fine sight wouldn't I? decking myself out with trinkets . . .

'But I saw her touch the necklace with the tip of one finger, very lightly, very gently — the way a woman touches something precious . . .

'Well — that's how she felt about Barbara, I believe, and I always shall.'

'And did Barbara — die?' Leonie ventured.

'No! She's living on her own and

working in London. She fell in love — desperately in love — with a man who was a Londoner, and a summer visitor here for the fishing. And when he came to tell Mrs. Langley that he wanted to marry Barbie, she insulted him and turned him out of the house — '

Leonie gasped.

'Oh, how appalling! *Why?* Just because she wanted her daughter to marry a Cumberland man?'

Ruth made a vague movement of her shoulders.

'None of us have ever known. Mrs. Langley utterly refused to say a word on the subject — except that she once said to Martin 'He was rotten to the core. I saved her from him . . . '

'Two days afterwards, Barbie did — what you did, Leonie . . . left a note for her mother and ran away — '

'To *him?*'

'No, definitely not. She made that quite clear. That makes it all the queerer, in a way . . . She got herself a job she got a lodging somewhere. She writes home at intervals, impersonal letters, a *stranger's* letters . . . I believe a complete melodramatic break couldn't hurt and infuriate her mother more . . . maybe not as much . . . '

* * *

. . . *Ostriches — that's what they* are, Janet Langley told herself grimly and bitterly. She was putting away a load of freshly laundered sheets and pillow-cases in the high linen-cupboard.

. . . Heads in the sand. Think a body hasn't the use of their eyes . . .

Never exchange a word anyone mightn't shout from the housetops. Never caught holding hands . . . or snatching a kiss . . .

But I've seen the way Martin's eyes follow that girl about. And I've seen the look in them.

. . . *She* won't give him a thought, not she. Of course not. To Miss Leonie Elwood, my son's no more than a working farmer, rough and uncouth.

But I'll not have him all upset and put about . . . and just when the winter lambing's due to start . . . He's lost his head, the fool — my Mart, that any girl in three parishes round would give her eyes to get. And when she's gone back to her fine London friends he'll be moody and hard to handle . . . and all her fault. It was a bad day that brought her here. I knew it from the first.

Well, go she will, and go she must. And before Mart gets wind of it, either.

There was a sudden fear in Janet's eyes.

. . . What if the girl falls in love with him in spite of all the difference there is in their ways of living and everything else? She'll never see a man more likely to catch a girl's fancy, than Martin . . . be he who he may . . . He's his father over again . . .

A spasm of almost physical pain contracted Janet's face. Without knowing it, she pressed the fingers of one hand against her breast.

This Leonie Elwood doesn't give a thought to anything except what she wants or doesn't want. Look at the way she's thrown her marriage away like a — like a used matchstick. If she takes a mad fancy to him, she'll get him in spite of her folks . . . In spite of *me* . . .

And then, what's to do? A soft, useless city girl, reared in wealth and luxury — what manner of wife would she make for a farmer? Break his heart, ruin his life, and leave him, soon or late — I wouldn't put it past her. She's thrown over one man already.

Or else — Mart would end by leaving *here*, where he belongs, and going to London with her.

It shall not happen, said Janet fiercely to herself as she shut the cupboard door.

4

'The telephone wires are mended,' Martin announced as he came into the house after trudging to and from the village.

'I know,' Ruth said indifferently. 'Your mother is on the line in the office at this minute.'

Martin felt some surprise. Although Janet had her finger in every transaction of Felstead's, the office work was left to Robert and himself, as a general rule.

Afterwards, he realised that it was some instinct, some premonition, which impelled him across the stone-floored hall to the office door. The door was not quite shut. He heard her voice, raised slightly, with impatience in the tone:

'Kingston one-one-three-o . . . I said *Kingston* . . . KING . . . oh, you've got it? about time, too — '

The repeated name sounded a small, sharp hammer in Martin's brain. KINGSTON . . . Suddenly he saw it: in sharp black letters, name and number, flashing from the Elwood vans as they rolled through the country.

And in the same instant another picture shot across Martin's memory. The week of the great agricultural exhibition at Olympia, when he and Robert had both gone south to London for it.

Martin had lost his elder brother for over an hour, in the huge and crowded hall. And found him, at last, standing enthralled, absorbed, and in deep conversation, at the stand where farm machinery was displayed, under the single, sufficient name, ELWOOD.

'Man, where've you been?' Martin demanded unnecessarily and in exasperation. 'You've missed the ring, d'you know that? I've had to show the ram myself . . . and we've won a First.'

Robert nodded absently at the sound of his brother's heated voice. He said,

'Mart — I've got a card from Mr. Carlow — ' he indicated the groomed, alert young man who was on the stand, 'and I can go out and look over the factory. It's on the Kingston Bypass . . . '

. . . KINGSTON 1130. And his mother was calling that number.

Martin pushed the door wide and strode into the room.

'Mother, what are you doing?' he asked sternly.

Janet, the receiver held to her ear, looked at him defiantly. Not a flicker of embarrassment went across her face. She was furious at the interruption; that was all.

'Be quiet,' she muttered. And then, 'Hullo? *Hullo*? Kingston? Is that Kingston? — '

Martin plucked the receiver from her fingers, replaced it, kept his hand upon it.

'How dare you?' Janet cried. 'Nearly ten minutes it's taken me to get through, and now — '

'You are ringing the Elwood factory,' Martin said with an ominous calm. 'What for?'

Janet tightened her lips. Tossed her grizzled head. Glared at him.

'I said, what for?' Martin repeated. 'Or shall I tell you? . . . '

'Have you lost your mind?' his mother burst out. 'Yes! that's just what you *have* done, Martin Langley . . . Lost your mind, gone clean daft, over a girl you never saw till close on a week ago.

'Oh, I've seen what's going on! And now the wires are up again, and I'm getting through to her father's works, and letting 'em know where she is and that the sooner she leaves here, the better.

'Listen to me, for a change, Mother. Leonie is the girl I'll make my wife, or I'll go unwed all my days. And no one — not even you — is going to put her out of this house till she's ready to go. That decision is for her to make and nobody else. And it's for her to tell her

86

parents where she's been.'

'Mart — what's come to you?' There was something desperate in Janet's rasping voice. 'I'll allow you — or any man, for that matter — could lose their head over her. She's — she's pretty,' said Janet lamely, inadequately, and as though the word stuck in her throat. 'And she's a — she's a kind, soft-spoken lass . . . I've nought to say against Leonie for herself . . . But do you think she'd look at *you?*

'Why, this very house makes her shudder,' said Janet bitterly. 'She's perished with cold, half the time . . . And the land frightens her. She's a girl used to soft living and big money and gay doings.

'You're a man whose folk have owned and farmed this land, time out o' mind. Ruth — even Ruth, with all her bookish notions, has said over and over again that Felstead, a house like Felstead, is like something out of a history book . . . a Cumberland history-book.

'But for Leonie, you're a farmer,

nothing more. She'll *laugh*, when she's among her own people again! It'll make a good story — the way she sheltered from the storm at a farm in the fells, and the son of the house went daft about her . . . '

'If you are so sure of that,' Martin said levelly, 'why are you so wild to get her out of the house?'

Janet flinched. Then she retorted vehemently. 'Because I'm taking no chances. She *could* take a mad fancy to you — and she's childish enough and light-headed enough to feel that it was worth losing her father's money, worth anything — while the fancy lasted. And that'd be worse than all. She'd soon tire of playing at being a farmer's wife. Or give you no peace, trying to get you to go her way, not yours.

'So now you know,' she ended breathelessly.

'I know what I've always known,' Martin rejoined, 'that you can't rest unless you're managing the lives of every soul in Felstead.

'And where has it got you, Mother? You drove Barbie away — '

Janet gave a sharp cry.

'It's a lie. It's a wicked lie. I saved her from spoiling her whole life — '

'Maybe. I wouldn't know anything about that. All I know is, that Barbie was the light of this house and you put it out,' Martin said briefly. 'Well, Mother, you're not going to do that to me. If Leonie ever comes to feel she can marry me, she will be my wife. And if things are made uncomfortable and unwelcoming for her here — then my wife and I will move into one of the Felstead cottages.'

'That'd be a fine home for her!' Janet jeered.

'It would be a happy one, at any rate. And if it came to that, then I would put every labour-saving gadget and every comfort into it that any woman could wish for.

'However — time enough to be thinking about such things . . . All I'm saying here and now, is; if you try to interfere with me and with Leonie, Mother, it's you that will regret it . . . '

He went out of the room.

Janet sat as though turned to stone.

Martin knew his mother too well to have any hope that the shock of this outspoken interview would change her plans in any degree. No child of hers — possibly no human being — had even spoken to her as he had spoken. But she would go on her own inflexible way.

'Where's Leonie?' he asked Ruth.

'Giving the children their lessons. Martin — is anything wrong? You look — queer — '

'No more so than usual,' he said grimly. 'Mother's on the warpath, Ruthie. I found her trying to telephone to the Elwood works in London — to report Leonie's whereabouts.'

Ruth gasped.

'Oh — oh, she's *guessed*?'

'It seems so.'

'Mart, it's frightful. What are you going to do?'

'Warn Leonie, of course.'

He went upstairs and found them deep in some handicraft which involved a good deal of water, paints, and paste, and Leonie's dark head bent over the satisfying mess between the two small heads.

Leonie's eyes widened and a startled, apprehensive look flashed into her face as she saw him.

'Martin — has something happened? Is Ruth all right?'

He nodded.

'Can I have a word with you? Come outside, will you?'

She rose and came out and Martin shut the door.

'Listen, my dear,' he said tensely. 'I've just come upon my mother, putting through a trunk call to your father's factory — to get a message to him saying you're here. I stopped the call; but you'd better know — '

Leonie gazed at him, bewildered.

'But why? Why, all of a sudden?' Then her face flushed hotly. 'She's guessed? That's it, isn't it?'

Martin bent his head.

'I've left nothing unsaid,' he said briefly. 'But nothing will stop her.'

'It doesn't matter — really. I — I hardly realised that the snow has stopped ... of course I must be going — '

Such a look of desolation swept over Martin's strong, controlled face that a pang went through her.

'Martin — you knew I'd have to go sometime? It's just that — somehow, everything outside these walls seems to have — stood still, and I've lost count of time!' she said, trying to laugh and speak lightly.

No echoing smile lit his sombre face.

'Leonie — what are you going back to?'

'How do you mean? Oh — not what you're thinking,' she cried quickly. 'That's all over — for ever. But I've been a coward, Martin, and very silly. I see that now. I owe it to Alaric — and to Daddy and Mummie — to go back and face the music.

'I've behaved very badly, and they'll all be very angry in their different ways . . . I deserve it. But since I came here, I do at least know that — loving is something greater than that.'

Her voice shook, broke on a little sob.

Martin put out his arms. But Leonie took a step back, shook her head, threw out a hand to check him.

'No, no, please — don't — touch me, Martin. If you do, I shan't be able to — think straight!' she said breathlessly and childishly.

'You've just said that you realise what my love for you means,' he said slowly and deeply. 'So — one day, you'll come back, my little heart, my darling.'

'I don't know, I don't know!' she whispered wildly. 'It's too soon. It's too quick. I must go — I must — '

'Leonie — ' Martin said.

And as though the sound of her name were some inevitable, irresistible call, a summons, she yielded, she flew into his arms and clung to him, sobbing.

'You do love me?' he said against her lips.

'I do, yes, I do! It must be love — because — '

'Because of what, my darling?'

'So many things!' she got out. 'I never felt — I never knew — '

She threw back her head and faced him, her brimming eyes brave and unashamed while the blood glowed in her wet cheeks.

'All this time,' said Leonie, unsteadily, 'all these endless, endless days — when you promised you wouldn't say anything — to show what you — what *we* felt — nor even touch me . . . I've *ached* for you, Martin . . . I've never felt that for anyone before, in my life. What made it — easy, in a way — to let myself get engaged to Alaric, was what I tried to say just now: he's a very cool, reserved, sort of person . . . and I was glad! I didn't want him to be anything else . . .

'I don't believe,' she added with an air of sheer discovery, 'I knew anything at all about — loving — till I met you . . . '

'Then, my little lass,' said Martin, 'what are we waiting for? . . . Yes, yes, I agreed you must go home. But I'll go with you. We'll face the music together.'

Leonie shook her head.

'Martin — Martin darling — I don't know how to say it — '

'I'll say it for you,' he said gravely, gently, his eyes looking into hers. 'It would mean facing — Mother, and all the mistrust and fear and bitterness she feels? Yes, I know, love, I know.

' . . . It would not need to be the nightmare it seems to you, Leonie. I wouldn't let it be. I've already had words with Mother about it and I told her just what I had in mind if you did come to feel that you could marry me . . . Just trust me. I would not let you live here in this house, if she couldn't change her attitude and her ways.

'So — go back, my heart. And take

all the time you need. Forget all about me — if you can . . . ' He touched her wet eyelids with his lips.

'You know I never can — '

'I pray you never can,' Martin amended quietly. 'I shall love you all my life, Leonie — but if ever you come back to me — come freely, come with joy . . . '

* * *

Ruth went into the bedroom where Leonie was packing. Leonie looked up from an open suitcase at the other girl's distressed and embarrassed face.

'Don't look like that! I would have had to leave anyway, once the roads were safe.'

'It's a shocking way to treat you, though,' Ruth protested unhappily. 'I feel it's a sort of slur on Felstead. We north-country people pride ourselves on being hospitable — '

'Don't bother about that,' Leonie said cheerfully.

'Ruth — it's Martin who's going to be hurt by all this. After all, I go home to my own people, and however much upset they are, they — won't be as hard on me as I deserve, really. But he stays here, without me — and he'll have his mother to bear as well as that — '

Ruth thought swiftly: You're growing up, my dear. If you can think of Martin before yourself — you're growing up.

'Martin is the only one who has ever been able to handle his mother. Leonie — if you can say that — you must care for him? A little?'

'Did you guess too — about us, I mean?'

'The very first minute I ever saw you together,' Ruth answered simply.

'I suppose,' Leonie said slowly, 'it was very stupid of me to imagine that it wouldn't — well, show! It was all so shatteringly sudden and quick, you see? And I didn't know where I was or what was happening to me . . .

'You say, do I care, Ruth? I love him as I've never loved anybody in the world . . . I know that, now. But — can't you see how terribly difficult it all is?'

'Of course I see it. Difficult for Martin as well as you, Leonie — '

'But that's what I've just been saying! When I'm gone, he — '

'I mean, if you come back,' Ruth said bluntly.

Leonie coloured, stared. Tears came into her eyes 'You mean — '

'My dear,' Ruth said more gently, 'Martin is a real brother to me. He talks to me . . . His mind is full of the sacrifice he's asking of you, if you marry him. He's full of plans for taking care of you . . . for finding a separate home . . . and making it comfortable . . . He's asked me about the things I used to take part in before I got married — the Amateur Dramatic Society at Clegshaw, the Music Club. There's a lot of what highbrow people call Cultural Interests here in the north,' Ruth said with a twinkle of amusement in her nice brown eyes.

'Mart is thinking about what you'd give up, what you'd miss, if you come to take up life here, as his wife.

'But what about the other side of it, Leonie?

'No one could deny that Mother Langley has behaved very badly; but at least it's only natural that she should see *that* side. Martin's roots are here in Felstead. And someday, he'll be Master of Felstead — because,' Ruth drew a quick deep breath, 'I don't know how and I don't know when, but some day I am going to *get* my Robert out of it and into the work and the life he wants . . . '

'The question is, what is Martin risking, in wanting you for his wife?'

Affronted colour flamed into Leonie's face.

'Robert risked a lot when he wanted you,' she returned unsteadily. 'You can't have *wanted* to marry a farmer? You were a trained school-teacher. You liked — music, and acting — I don't know a single thing about music, I never read anything except the new novels, and acting only means going to the theatre, for me — '

Ruth laughed.

'Bless you for those few kind — ! But it's not at all the same thing. I am Cumberland-born, my lass. And I come of working folk, even if — '

'So do I!' Leonie interrupted. 'Everybody seems to think I don't realise that. But I do. Mummie — ' she hesitated, went on courageously, 'likes to forget it, I think. 'But I don't. When Daddy started — '

'Yes, yes, I know,' Ruth interrupted in her turn. 'But it's still a different thing altogether, Leonie. You've lived in the sort of sphere which we all know from the glossies. A wife can help her husband or — wreck him. I've seen it before.'

'So you think that's what I'd do to Martin?' Leonie's eyes were sparkling with challenge.

'All I'm trying to say, is, face facts, Leonie? For your own sake, and Martin's sake. And don't be angry with me — '

'I'm not,' Leonie said, absently, as though it were of less than no importance. 'But I know one thing: I love Martin.'

'Well, thank God you can say that!' Ruth said. 'Here's the address of the café where Barbara works. Do look her up? Find out how things are going with her, and let us know — let Martin know, anyway, or me.'

'I will, gladly,' Leonie said, folding the piece of paper into her handbag.

Ruth had more than one reason for putting Leonie in touch with Barbara. News of his sister might quite possibly give Martin an excuse for going south; if the two girls should become friendly, he would see Leonie again . . . And, in her own mind, Ruth felt, pessimistically, that Leonie might falter in her faith towards Martin once she found herself away from his world and back in the world that was hers.

Early next morning, Leonie went to say good-bye to Martin's mother. She had been nerving herself for this encounter ever since she woke in the grey darkness. Now, on the threshold of the stone-floored office, all apprehension dropped from the girl's mind and nerves. She felt calm, and in some indefinable way, adequate.

Janet fixed Leonie with a perfectly blank, expressionless gaze.

'I have come to say good-bye, Mrs. Langley. And to thank you — to try to thank you — for all you've done for me.'

'I want no thanks from anyone,' Janet said tersely. 'And I expect none. You'll be telling your father and mother, I make no doubt, that even if I took you into my house I turned you out of it . . .'

'No, I shan't say anything like that,' Leonie said. 'And I don't blame you for wanting to get rid of me, Mrs. Langley. There have been times in the last few days when I almost wished I'd never come here — '

'You say that?' Janet exclaimed, amazed.

'So, you see, we're of one mind — to some extent!' Leonie said with a quivering smile.

'Well — it's been unlucky,' Janet said grimly. 'But you'll have forgotten this place and everyone and everything in it, before you've been back among your own folk very long.'

'That will never happen,' Leonie said quietly. 'You know that, I think. And there's nothing you can say to me that I haven't thought already. I'm not the kind of person Martin needs as a wife. He's not the kind of man I could ever have imagined myself as marrying. But I know one thing; we can never get away from each other . . . even if we never set eyes on one another again for the rest of our lives . . . '

'You don't know what you're saying. That's crazy talk — '

There was a sharp sound in Janet's voice.

'I daresay you're right, Mrs. Langley. Loving isn't a reasonable thing . . . I've found that out.'

She bent her clear, unwavering eyes on the working face before her.

'Can't you help us, instead of — fighting us?' she asked suddenly and simply.

'The best help I can give either of you is to say, go away, Leonie Elwood, go away and never come back,' Janet said hoarsely. 'No good can come of it, girl, I'm telling you.'

'It seems to me there's not much happiness for him — or for anyone — in this house, as it is,' Leonie said. '*You're* the unhappiest person I've ever met, I think — '

Janet put a hand to her throat as though something choked her.

'Aye! I know what you mean. You say unhappy, but you mean hard, bitter, twisted . . . It would never enter your head to wonder if there was any cause — '

'I've wondered nearly every time I look at you,' Leonie countered.

'Have you? Then I'll tell you,' said Janet Langley. 'And that's something

I've never told another soul.

'You said just now, that you and Martin can never be quit of one another — not if you never saw one another again. You're young, you're in love, you're talking wild because you're all worked-up . . .

'But I know the truth of what you've said. I've lived with it for more than half my life . . . '

She was silent for a moment, then she went on abruptly, 'I was a plain-looking lass, always. Even from a child. And as early as I knew anything at all, I knew it.' She lifted her bitter, knife-keen gaze to Leonie's intent and listening face.

'I had a sister who was the prettiest thing in these parts . . . Mollie was a bright, laughing lass, and the boys were round her like wasps round a honey-pot. I grew a sullen, crabbed girl; or so they called me . . .

'Simon Langley came courting from Felstead. Courting my sister. And I — loved him.' Janet's thin lips stammered and seemed to writhe on the unaccustomed word. 'You think Martin's a fine figure of a man, and so he is; but you never saw his father . . .

'Mollie and he were to be wed in the spring. And a month before the wedding, she died . . . There was sickness in the valley that winter, I reckon it was some poisonous sort of influenza.

'She died. And Simon was like — ' Janet paused, flinching, quivering as she opened a long-ago wound with her own ruthless fingers — ' like a dead man, going about . . . his eyes — Martin has his eyes — looking like the open eyes of a blind man. He was alone here, at Felstead, except for the farm-hands, and the old soul who came up from the village to do for him. The two men would talk in the tavern, in the evenings . . . said they reckoned 't'master' was going out of his mind . . . Bye-and-bye, old Sarah stopped going up there; she said she was feared what she'd find, any day . . .

'So — one day, I went up to Felstead — and what was said between Simon and me never passed my lips and never shall . . . We were wed . . . And from that day to this, I've served Felstead.

'He died when Robert was ten years old. I lived for ten years with a man who was everything in this world to me; *and whose heart was in my sister's grave.* I've lived for twenty years since — *and he's still what he was to me.* I've gone starved and hungering all my life, Leonie Elwood.

'What are *you* crying for?' Janet wound up, sharply.

Leonie leaned against the cold, whitewashed wall, the tears streaming down her cheeks. She shook her head wordlessly.

'My girl Barbara — you'll have heard all about her, I'll be bound? Barbara was a baby when her father died. I watched her grow more like him every year of her life . . . me, with a daughter as *sightly* as you are — that was a thing to wonder at,' Janet said with a bitter laugh. 'Well, she's gone. And now you've come to set this house by the ears, this house that I've given everything I have, to build up and keep going.

'I tell you, a fair face in man or woman is a curse — not to them, oh no, never to them! they only have to flick a finger or throw a smile, and you're bound to them, body and soul, and for life . . . And the rest of us must slave alone in the dark . . . and be like to die of hunger and thirst for what we can never have, never . . .

'*Go away*, girl. Get from here, before you do more harm than you've done already.'

Leonie went to the rigid, bitter figure and stooped. Her wet cheek touched Janet's. She kissed her, and fled.

Robbie and Janey cast themselves on Leonie crying loudly.

'I don't want you to go away! Why are you?'

'When'll you come back? You *mus'* come back, Leonie — '

She went to her knees on the stone

floor of the hall and gathered them into her arms and sobbed as she kissed the small heads burrowing into her neck, and ran out to the car.

Martin sat at the wheel.

'I'll drive you as far as the cross-roads,' he said briefly.

At the signpost, he drew up. They sat looking at one another, in the utter silence and solitude of the white hills rising and sweeping about them. And Martin took her in his arms.

'Don't cry, love — ' he muttered, uselessly.

He held her, without speaking until the storm of tears was spent.

'I'll be all right,' Leonie said, trying to smile at him. 'You — you get back, now.'

He got out of the car, and Leonie slipped into the driving-seat.

'God bless you — ' she whispered. 'I'm not going to say good-bye — '

Martin stood there, a solitary figure in the white expanse of silence as the car vanished over the hill.

5

The next morning, Leonie drove down the grey and beautiful stretch of the Thames, and drew up before Embankment Court. The blackened slush which is the ugly aftermath of snow in a city had been cleared away.

For the first time since she escaped into the white, snow-locked world which lay behind her, she gave a thought to what day of the week it was. Sunday! . . . Of course! It was Sunday.

And her father would be at home . . .

The lift stopped. Leonie stepped out into the warmth and silver-rose light of the hallway and put her key into the door of the flat.

At the end of the long drawing-room sliding doors shut off a small ante-room which was usually known simply as 'the Little Room', which was used as a breakfast room. Voices came to Leonie as she made her way down the long expanse of carpet which had never seemed so long . . . She slid back the smooth, soundless panels of the ivory-coloured doors, and saw her parents sitting at breakfast, the Sunday papers deployed among the silver and delicate china and flowers.

Albert Elwood was a solid figure of a man with a face that was kindly as well as shrewd. He had been distinctly good-looking as a young man, he was impressive-looking now.

Gladys Elwood was the type of middle-aged woman whom you will see shopping in the more expensive and less popular stores, any day of the week. They are beautifully, unobtrusively groomed from head to foot. And everything which they wear is of the best.

Gladys Elwood had been a plump, chubby girl, she was a plump, ample woman. She sat at breakfast in a mulberry-coloured house-coat of corded silk, there were small rose-bloomed pearls in the lobes of her ears below the close set iron-grey hair, and as she re-filled her husband's coffee cup the single great diamond on her hand flashed in the faint winter sunlight.

There was a moment, one of those timeless moments, of complete silence. Gladys Elwood's face filled slowly with angry colour. Her plump, ringed hands made a hopeless gesture.

'*Really*, my dear girl — *really*, Leonie — '

Albert Elwood got heavily to his feet, and pushed a chair to the table.

'Sit down Leo. You'd better have some coffee — '

'Coffee!' his wife echoed. She was trembling, Leonie saw. Her voice rose on the word.

'Give her some coffee,' Albert bade his wife in the same impersonal manner. 'We don't know how far she's been driving — and in this cold' —

'Daddy — ' Leonie broke out on a sort of wail, 'don't! Say anything you want to — I deserve it all, I know —

112

but don't treat me as if I — as if I — as if I hadn't come home!' she finished lamely.

'It's rather late in the day to think of that, isn't it?' her mother said. 'A nice way you've treated us putting us to shame before every soul we know . . . and making us a laughing stock among thousands whom we don't know and who don't know us. I shall never hold up my head again — '

'Mummie, that's not fair. It's not even true. I've been a coward, I've been silly, I've been selfish — but I've done nothing to make anybody ashamed — '

'You don't appear to realise quite what you have done, my girl,' her father said stonily. His cold manner was in contrast to his wife's trembling fury. 'You've been our first thought, always. We've given you everything any girl could wish for. You've so taken it all for granted, that you've lost sight of the most important thing we've given you, Leonie.

'And that's the position, the standing, the place in the world, which belongs to you.

'It's meant a lifetime of hard work, getting there. Hard work for both your mother and me.'

'And now what happens? You pick and choose for nearly three years, you refuse offers any girl would have jumped at; at last you take Alaric Brooke. And we couldn't be better pleased.

'And then, at the last minute — the very last minute — you behave like a girl who's suddenly lost her mind. Rush off into the blue, leaving silly notes behind you.'

Leonie opened her lips as her father paused. But her mother rushed in before she could utter a word.

'And as for Alaric — what do you suppose *he's* feeling A man at the beginning of a political career. Only time will show how much damage you've done to him. Already one of those low, scandalous papers has a sneering paragraph about lovely young bride unable to face future . . . why? . . . All sorts of vile rumours will go round, of course.'

'Mummie — please — please — for pity's sake — '

'Pity? How much pity have you shown, Leonie? The whole Brooke connection will cold-shoulder us now. I can't face those people and hear them whispering and watch them smiling and shrugging . . .

'And what do you imagine your father and I have gone through, not even knowing where you were until that farm-woman got on the telephone and said you were just leaving for home? What in the name of sense took you all that way to the north, anyway?'

'I thought of Aunt Ellie, at Carlisle. Or even of old Margit, in Edinburgh. And then I remembered that Aunt Ellie would be on her way south — '

Gladys gave a sound perilously akin to a snort.

'Yes! And a fine state Ellie was in

when she found what had happened. Travelling half-across England for nothing but a scandal . . .

'She'd brought you her pearls. And a cheque for a hundred pounds. She tore up the cheque and you'll certainly never see the pearls.'

Leonie said slowly, painfully, because her throat was swelling with a rising flood of tears.

'I suppose — that really was why — I thought of them both. Aunt Ellie was always sweet and — kind to me.'

'And Margit — ' Leonie stopped. The childish memories of that old Scottish nurse, soft of voice, quiet and gentle of manner, Margit, who made the nursery a haven, Margit who always made you feel safe, threatened to break down her control.

'I'm sorry Mummie — I'm sorry, Daddy. But — I *tried* to tell you that I wasn't sure of myself, about marrying Alaric. You wouldn't understand. I tried to talk to him — and he just smiled and told me not to worry and it would be all right once we were away by our-selves — '

Her father cleared his throat.

'If you felt so strongly, why couldn't you have broken off the engagement in the usual way? A notice in the papers — '

'I suppose,' Leonie said, a flare of pent feeling breaking through the strained pallor of her young face, 'because I knew there would be just the kind of — scene — I've come back to, now. And I just couldn't take it . . . Well, I've had to take it, anyway.'

She moved slowly to the door feeling a sagging exhaustion from head to foot.

She stood at the windows of her own lovely bedroom staring into the green enclosure which lay behind the block of flats. It had once been a deep Chelsea garden, and it was perfectly preserved. There were stone troughs and carved stone urns on the bricked terrace, bright patches of colour because they were filled with winter cherries.

Leonie felt as though she were numb

from a battering of blows. But one thing forced its way through the numbness like pain. The truth drove its way into her consciousness.

They were angry, and they had the right to be angry. And when Mummie was upset, she always said more than she meant. But — but — this concentration on hurt pride and endangered ambitions was something which she herself had never expected. She had expected them to be hurt in their feelings, to upbraid her for hurting Alaric's feelings. Not to be told that she had injured her family's position . . . their social standing . . .

There was no mention of pain for Alaric. Only that a young politician shouldn't be involved in gossip or scandal . . .

What more could they have said if I'd done something really shameful? . . .

It's unfair! It's also ridiculous!

Oh — they love me dearly, I know that. But why doesn't anybody — anybody — stop to think that *I* went through misery before I took this way out?

A voice echoed suddenly in her ears. A harsh, gruff voice with a north country accent and drawl: *Girls have run away from their wedding before now . . .*

The only person who didn't see it as a crime, as anything outlandish, even, was the woman who was her one enemy. Martin's mother cursed the day which had brought her to Felstead, but she didn't think her mad — or bad! — for running away . . .

★ ★ ★

I must be awfully naïve, Leonie thought. Her cheeks felt hot all over again from that brief conversation with Alaric across the telephone, as she sat beside him in his car, driving through the river suburbs.

She had taken up the receiver with a hand that shook. What would he say? Would he hang up as he recognised her voice? Would he be cold, distant, curt, in his own polished way?

Or almost anything. Not for Alaric's voice, perfectly calm and unruffled, saying, 'Leonie? Is that you? So you're back — '

She'd said breathlessly, 'Yes. And I — Alaric, I want to see you. I must talk to you, please!'

'Why not?' he returned cheerfully, evenly.

'Are you free tonight?' she asked.

'Well — the evening's not a good idea is it?' Alaric's voice came, consideringly, over the line. 'We'd better drive a bit out of town.'

Leonie suppressed an impulse to say that she'd had enough of driving in the country to last her for some time . . .

'Shall we say lunch, tomorrow?' Alaric resumed the subject. 'You can? Good! I'll call for you at twelve, then.'

As she hung up the truth flashed upon Leonie. Alaric was not going to suggest meeting at any of their usual rendezvous. They'd be seen . . . recognised . . . the tongues would start wagging again. Seen lunching or dining together, straight on the heels of a broken engagement.

And Alaric was a man whose London orbit was bound by a circle which seems limitless to those who are outside it and which is no larger than a village to those inside.

Leonie felt profoundly thankful that Alaric preserved a total silence, though it was nerve-racking. He slowed down as they came to a country hotel, a fine old white house set back in its trees.

'This looks possible, don't you think?'

'Yes — anywhere — ' Leonie said incoherently. 'Alaric — I must talk to you first — '

He turned in at the open gates, up the winding drive.

'Well — we'll go for a walk. If you're not cold?'

They walked into the secluded shrubbery, and down a short flight of steps into the deserted garden. Alaric smiled at her.

'My dear, don't look so upset!' he said kindly. Leonie gulped.

'I don't know where to begin — '

'Need you begin anywhere? Your letter explained — '

'But that's not enough!' she said feverishly. 'I want to beg your pardon, Alaric. I want to tell you how sorry — how wrong I know it was — to do it like that!'

'You needn't have put yourself to all this stress,' Alaric said in the same kindly, slightly detached tone. 'I understand, you know?'

Her eyes filled with tears.

'Oh — you're being too good — too generous — Oh Alaric — they say I've done you harm — in your career, I mean — '

'Who says so?' he asked quickly.

'My people — my mother, anyway. They say the papers will make a scandal out of it.'

'Listen, my dear child. Put that idea

out of your head, once and for all. Your mother has a rather exaggerated idea of the power of the press . . . '

Leonie saw more feeling in his cool, impervious eyes than she ever remembered.

'My poor, dear Leonie! I can see you've had a bad time! They were very much — upset, your people?'

'Very! Alaric — they seem to think I've embarrassed them as well,' Leonie said. 'They say — ' she hesitated. She searched for words which would not be too crude . . .

'They feel that people are going to — ostracise them, because of it. Especially — your parents and your friends.'

'Absolute nonsense!' Alaric said.

'Well, that's what I feel!' Leonie said, thankful and relieved. 'I mean — it can't be so important — to anyone except — ourselves. Can it?' she asked wistfully.

'Certainly not. Look, Leonie, I'll have a talk with your parents, if you like?'

'Will you? Will you really? That would be the one thing which might make them see things differently.

'Alaric — you're being so kind. Will you believe how much I hate hurting you?'

He took her arm and gave it a brief pressure.

'Let's say no more, shall we?'

Leonie felt queerly deflated . . .

I'm an ungrateful wretch! she told herself. It was a blessed relief to have Alaric take it all as he was taking it.

She should be feeling humbled with gratitude. But — could Alaric — could any man who was really in love be quite so — noble? Be quite so — cheerful? said a small voice in Leonie's inward ear . . .

Alaric Brooke was, in a word, a man whose emotions were never likely to gain the upper hand.

He cared, sincerely, for a lovely and most lovable girl, as far as it was in him to care for anything other than his career.

124

He disliked Gladys Elwood. And found her blatant snobbery embarrassing and exasperating. He was ready to smooth over an awkward situation with urbane *savoir faire* and genuine generosity. He was equally ready to maintain friendly relations with his ex-fiancée and he would have considered it vulgar and uncouth to do otherwise.

★   ★   ★

'I told you how it would be!' Janet said triumphantly to Ruth. 'I said, let that girl only get out of the house and things would settle down and be normal and sane again like they were before.'

Ruth said nothing, but went on with the hanging up of her baby son's nappies.

And Janet, who would ordinarily have goaded Ruth — or anyone else — until she got a reply (and the reply that she wanted), said nothing, either.

Because she knew quite well that her defiant assertions was not true . . .

On the surface, life at Felstead went on as usual. Martin exhibited no dark moods, no sullenness, and was as absorbed in the running of the farm as ever.

But his mother knew — and Ruth knew that she knew — that there was something different . . .

Martin had always possessed and shown the confidence which his older brother lacked. But now it showed itself more forcibly than ever and with a new quietness of complete assurance.

Martin had been the one to argue with his mother, before. Now there were no more arguments. Instead, he acted as he thought fit . . .

As for Janet Langley, she was afraid . . .

Afraid, never of her quiet son, but of this new manifestation of his force of character and a will-power as strong as her own.

Martin was taking his stand in the small things of everyday decision and management on the farm, because, from now on, he would take his stand in the large issues of his own life.

. . . And it was all due to 'that girl' . . .

The Saturday after Leonie left, Janet checked the week's accounts.

'Martin, what's this?' she demanded. 'You've put down Jim's wage as two pounds more than it is. How did you come to make such a slip?'

'It's no slip,' Martin returned calmly. 'I've spoken to you time and again about raising Jim, Mother. He's earned it, for one thing. With the rising cost of living, he needs it, for another. Do you want to get the name for the one skinflint wage-payer in these parts? If you do, it's goodbye to a chap like Jim. He's the best shepherd this side of Liddon Fell, and I can't afford to lose him.'

Janet crimsoned with anger. But before she could burst into speech, Martin had gone to the door. He said, over his shoulder, 'And while you're about it, you'd do well to raise

Georgina. They're man and wife, and if you lose one you'll lose both.'

On another day, the children came flying into the house from school, breathless with excitement.

'You're home early!' Janet commented.

'Yes!' Robbie gasped joyously. 'Uncle Mart came by in the new car, and he gave us a lift — Janey and me and Sally and Dick and the Renwick twins — all of us.'

Janet dried her hands, and went to the front door.

There stood a station wagon ... obviously not 'new', but shining with fresh paint and varnish. Martin, Robert and Jim were standing round it.

At the sight of Janet, Jim slouched away, Robert looked apprehensive and uneasy.

'Rob, take the children indoors,' Janet directed curtly.

'But, *Gran* — come and sit in the new car — ' Robbie protested.

His father said quickly, 'Come

indoors, you two — ' and took Janey's small hand.

Martin stood motionless, his eyes on his mother.

The two little faces fell. The excitement and delight drained from them, and Janey began to whimper.

Martin said, 'Don't fret, my lass. Nor you, Robbie. I'll take you in the car presently — '

'Before we have our tea?'

'Yes, before you have your tea.'

Satisfied, they trotted into the house. Then Janet turned on Martin.

'What's to do?' she said vehemently.

'Thanks, at any rate, for getting the children out of the way, Mother,' Martin said drily. 'I've bought this from Dan Cridley.'

'What possessed you to do such a thing?'

'It's more than time there was a decent car on the place. That old Ford is eating money in repairs — even if Robert does most of them.'

Janet knew that it was true. What

infuriated her was, that Martin had replaced the old car without consulting her.

'What did you give for it?'

'He wanted four hundred. I got him down to two hundred and fifty.'

'And who's paying that out, I'd like to know?'

'I wrote the cheque on the farm account, naturally. It's not my private car, Mother!'

'Isn't it? Isn't it?' she stormed. 'As though you'd have got it if you weren't thinking about that girl . . . coming back here . . . and the old Ford not good enough for *her* — '

Martin threw back his splendid head and laughed.

'Considering that Leonie's own car is a brand new Jaguar, that's funny! When Leonie comes here — ' there was a slight emphasis on the 'when' and Janet heard it — 'I shall get a smaller car for our own use, and not on the farm account, either.'

Janet flung away from him and went

into the house and slammed the door.

There was no arguing with Martin, she discovered, to her baffled fury. He simply walked away if she railed at him.

Her tyrannies, her interference, her 'management' went further even than usual, reaching out even to the children.

Matters reached something of a climax, when Janet came into the kitchen where Ruth was laying the big table for the high tea one evening, and found her talking to Robert and the children prancing about the table with faces of excitement. Robert was smiling, and Ruth's face was sparkling with pleasure.

' . . . I'll be rusty after all this while! but I'd love to be doing it again — '

'And so you should. I'm glad about this, dear — '

'Mummy says *we* can go, too! We can go and see it — '

'Certainly you shall. You and I will sit in the very front row and clap like mad every time Mummy is on the stage — '

'That'll be a nice help!' Ruth laughed. 'You'll be turned out of the hall.'

They became aware of Janet, looking on and listening.

Robert said in his nervous, placating manner, 'Great goings-on, Mother! The Enthwaite Players are going to give a play over at the Memorial Hall, and they want Ruth for their leading lady!'

'Oh, not quite that!' Ruth protested. 'The old lady's is really the most important part. But Meg is a nice part — '

'And when is all this play-acting to take place?' Janet asked, sitting down at the table.

'The play — it's called *The Distaff Side*, Mother — will be put on just before Christmas. But we shall start rehearsals this week.'

'Mrs. Drummond wants us to borrow as many of the dresses as possible. I wondered whether you would lend us — '

'Make the tea,' Janet commanded, interrupting. 'As for all this flummery,

I'll have naught to do with it. And nor will you, my girl. That sort of thing was all very well when you hadn't a home and children to keep you busy.'

'It'll all be in the evenings, naturally,' Ruth countered quietly, but with her colour rising and her eyes very bright. 'Everyone taking part is at work during the day.'

'The more fools, they, then, to clutter up the evenings with such nonsense. You've a young baby — or had you forgotten? I didn't work my hands to the bone looking after you, to have you gallivanting about the neighbourhood as soon as you were on to your feet, Ruth.'

The children were staring.

'Gran, Daddy's goin' to take *us* to watch!' Robbie announced.

'You get on with your tea, lad,' Janet bade him. 'That beats all,' she said to Robert. 'If you think I'd allow the children to be taken out at night when they should be in their beds, you're daft, Rob. We'll have no more of this tomfoolery, thank you.'

Janey raised a wail. Ruth put an arm round her.

'Hush darling. Everything will be quite all right — '

'And so it will,' Robert said quietly. And his quiet voice, was as much of a surprise as though he had shouted. 'Ruth will take part in this play, Mother. It's been over-long since she had anything of her own interests. And the children will come with me, to see it.'

The storm broke. Janet's angry voice rose, pouring out a stream of vituperation, while both children burst into frightened tears.

'Now look what you've done,' Ruth broke out, goaded beyond endurance. 'Mother — you've never made them cry before . . . '

Janet got up, and went up the walled stairs. They heard the door of her bedroom shut in the recesses of the house.

'It'll be all right,' Ruth said, wiping

Janey's eyes, while Robert took his little boy on his knee. 'She'll come down bye-and-bye and ignore the whole thing as if it had never happened. You know she will, Rob, dearie.'

Robert, stroking the small, dark head, had a strange look on his face; a look of white, tightened resolve . . .

'I reckon this is the end, Ruthie.'

'What do you mean? Rob — don't — '

'I'm not even sure — yet — what I do mean,' he confessed. 'But this can't go on. We'll get away, Ruth. We must. There's plenty of openings in Cumberland.'

'Life here just isn't worth it, the way things are. It's different for Martin — his heart's in it. Mine never was.'

'We'll start all over again!'

Ruth laid an arm about his neck and her cheek against his.

'Thank God!' she breathed.

6

It was queer, Leonie thought, how things settled down. A week ago, ten days ago, she was in a whirl of bewilderment, confronted by angry parents, faced, apparently, with a prospect of general disapproval, criticism, censure.

Now, the days went on exactly as usual.

A girl or two among her friends asked a few direct questions. There were some curious, enquiring looks. Otherwise the world went its way, undisturbed by the fact that the marriage between Alaric Brooke and Leonie Madeleine Elwood was not to take place . . .

Even the anger of her father and mother had simmered and died down. More rapidly after Alaric called on Albert Elwood in his private office.

Although the girl herself didn't

realise it, her parents knew a strange unaccustomed sensation as they watched her since her return. They were unsure of their idolised, distracting daughter for the first time.

And unsure of themselves . . .

Leonie was out of reach. Inaccessible. They felt it even though they could not express the feeling.

And then there was another reason for bewilderment. Alaric calm and friendly; nobody cutting and cold-shouldering; nobody, believe it or not, even extraordinarily *interested* in the earthquake which had shaken the Elwood family to its insecure foundations.

Much ado about nothing. Mountains out of molehills. The homely phrases buzzed uncomfortably in Gladys Elwood's mind. Was it possible that she'd been making a fool of herself?

And then, there was Albert's quoting of something which Alaric Brooke had said to him.

'Believe me, sir, the only injury to

anyone which can come from this affair, will come if you and her mother make too much of it . . . '

The earthquake had subsided. But the ground under their feet didn't feel as secure, as established, as it was before.

Leonie's father and mother felt a small, cold wind of doubt in their minds: was it possible that what had seemed of overwhelming importance hadn't the unique, the all-pervading value which they were so stubbornly convinced that it had?

For the first few days at home, once the atmosphere cleared and settled, Leonie felt nothing so acutely and intensely as the physical relief of being warm, comfortable, and among familiar things again!

And there were so many enjoyable things waiting for her! The things which Leonie had taken for granted, which were just a succession of scribbles in her engagement book.

An evening at the ballet. A cocktail

party at Rose Mowbray's — lights and voices and laughter and keen talk that never flagged. The Webberburn's dance.

With a prick of shamefaced contrition Leonie admitted to herself that dances hadn't been so much fun during her brief engagement . . . Alaric did not care for dancing and was an uninspiring partner . . . on this occasion Leonie was danced off her feet.

Suddenly, and without warning, the sense of well-being, of enjoyment, evaporated . . . Leonie was walking down the embankment towards the flats. It was a day of winter sunlight flashing on the water, of gulls wheeling, of tugs hooting with that immemorial sound which tug at some hidden fibre in your heart and calls you to adventure . . .

As though a blow struck her, as though a knife pierced her, Leonie wanted Martin . . . Wanted him with an overwhelming longing.

She stood still, turning to rest her

arms on the stone parapet, looking out over the river.

Martin . . . Martin . . . I want you. Nothing else matters.

I don't know how I can ever learn — your way of life. You could never learn mine — and I wouldn't even ask you to try. It *would* be murder. Murder of everything that is you . . .

I'm not afraid of your mother any more. Only terribly sorry for her. You can't be afraid of anyone once you're sorry for them. But she hates me — it would be a frightful business, trying to win her, trying to live with her . . .

I don't know . . . I don't know . . . I only know I miss you so that I can hardly breathe . . .

She opened her handbag to take out a handkerchief and pressed it against her trembling lips and touched her smarting eyelids. As she put it back, she caught sight of a piece of paper folded into the pocket. Leonie had a certain fastidious daintiness about many things, and among them, about the interior of her numerous handbags. She did not let oddments accumulate. Frowning, now she picked out the bit of paper.

On it, in Ruth's neat handwriting, was,

Barbara Langley
    Café Carrib
        Weldon Street.
        South Kensington.

Barbara . . . Leonie had forgotten all about Barbara. There rushed over that invariable, unreasoning impulse of every woman in love: to clutch at any contact with anybody who can be said to belong to the one whom you love . . .

She would go and see Barbara. She would go directly after lunch.

Leonie smiled to herself as she set out. The address surprised her, and amused her, too, a little bit. The Cafés Carrib were a chain of small, new restaurants which had sprung up in London like brilliant jungle toadstools.

They served delicious snacks and incomparable coffee, and they were very expensive indeed . . .

Leonie had heard from Ruth that Janet Langley was affronted and humiliated by the fact that her girl had taken a job 'in a café'. Well — Barbara certainly hadn't landed herself in any carter's pull-in . . .

The Café Carrib was empty except for two elderly women who were sitting over after-lunch coffee and cigarettes, and a group of swarthy young men who were talking animatedly in some foreign language unknown to Leonie.

Ruth had said, 'You can't miss Barbie. Rather tall, and as slim as you are, and golden hair — and dark eyes. She had her hair cut short and styled — (and was Mother Langley livid!) but it still tosses into sort of halo round her head . . . '

But the only two young women in the café were the dark-haired girl at the cash desk and another brunette with an olive skin, wearing a bizarre plastic apron over an emerald-green woollen skirt.

'Yes, Madame?' she said enquiringly and with an accent which Leonie's trained ear registered as part-of-the act.

'I am looking for a Miss Langley — a Miss Barbara Langley — who works here.'

The brunette shrugged, and looked uncertainly at the cashier.

'Miss Langley went sick,' the other young woman supplied pleasantly but indifferently. 'She was away for too long. We couldn't hold the job open. She won't be coming back.'

Leonie's heart sank.

'Can I get her address? Where she is living, I mean?'

The girl shook her head. 'I'm sorry! We don't keep any records once anyone quits.'

Leonie went out into the grey street. So, this was what it was like — the thing that books and plays and magazine stories were always describing. The frightful *alone-ness* of a great city. If you were a total stranger, a newcomer without a single link, you could drop from sight like a stone down a well . . .

She braced herself suddenly. Ruth said a letter had come from Barbara the very day I turned up at Felstead. Evidently she didn't say a word about being ill . . . but at least they must have the address.

Directly she got home Leonie wrote to Ruth:

'Dear Ruth,

Please keep this letter to yourself, if you can. I went to the café to see Barbara, today. But they tell me she was off because of illness, and it must have been before her last letter home because they spoke of not being able to keep the job open for so long. As she apparently did not mention being ill in her letter, it sounds as though she must be better?

Anyway, send me her address as soon as you can, please.'

She sat, pondering, pen in hand. If she said anything more — no! it was too soon . . .

She ended,

'Give my love to the children.

Leonie.'

Ruth's answer came two days later.

'Dear Leonie,

By good luck, I met the postman in the road and got your letter without anyone knowing. It is a shock to hear that Barbie has been ill. Her last letter did come the very day you arrived here, and it was shorter than usual and said she had no news.

Mother Langley was upset when she read it, but no more than usual. She is always upset when she gets a letter from Barbara. I don't think I ever told you that after B. first wrote saying she had a job, Mother Langley told Martin to write a cheque and send it to her. Well, Barbie sent it back to Martin and wrote that she could look after herself and didn't need charity . . .

It hurt her mother, badly. And I'm pretty sure that she worries exceedingly about Bar . . .

Now she's been in one of her worst moods all this week because no letter has come since the day you got here. There's no contenting her! The letters make her angry when they do come or when they don't . . .

Barbara wrote from 7 Tadworth Street, Fulham.

The children send their love.

R.L.

P.S. I wish you had sent some news about yourself and how things have gone since you got back.'

Leonie shrank, in some way, from the postscript. No — no — she must wait. That sudden overwhelming longing for Martin wasn't enough. She must be sure. Sure of so many things.

Tadworth Street, in a winter twilight,

was a grim terrace of those London houses which were solid three-storied villas once upon a time, with pillars flanking the front door and a flight of steps dropping to a square of London grass which could be called a front garden. They had a dingy look, the pillars were flaking, the grass was muddy. But there hung about them, like rags in a wind, the remnants of past prosperity and solidity.

Leonie tugged at an iron bell. A door opened in the paved area below the steps and there peered up at her an apple-cheeked damsel in a thick sweater and slacks.

'Hello!' she said cheerfully. 'Who do you want?'

'A Miss Langley — '

'Right-ho! I'll pop up and open the door.' She appeared a minute later.

'You jerk the bell once for the basement, twice for the ground floor, and so forth,' she explained. 'And whoever it is you're jerking for comes and lets you in.'

She considered the visitor with frank interest.

'I know Barbara Langley,' she volunteered. 'She's been ill, poor kid. And she doesn't seem to know a soul — '

'Has she seen a doctor, do you know?'

'Shouldn't think so. She went down with 'flu and she doesn't seem to have picked up. We all did a bit of this and that for her, of course — there are five of us here, three foreign students, and Barbara, and me. We got in a bit of food, and made her bed, and so forth,' said Apple-cheeks breezily. 'She's second floor — door facing the stairs.'

'She's in, then? She's got back from — wherever she's working?'

'Bless you, she hasn't been working since she first went sick. She's as wobbly as a new kitten!'

'Oh — good heavens!' Leonie murmured. 'Thank you so much — I'll go straight up.'

She went up the stairs to the dim landing above and knocked at the door.

'Come in!' a voice said.

Leonie got a general impression of a divan bed and a mixture of cheap modern-style furniture and clumsy old-fashioned pieces. There was a noisy gas-fire.

Barbara was sitting on a cushion on the floor before the fire, her shoulders propped against the foot of the divan, a book in her lap, and a work-basket beside her. She looked at Leonie enquiringly.

'Miss Langley?' Leonie said.

'Yes.' Barbara got to her feet and Leonie exclaimed, 'Oh, don't please! I know you've been ill — '

'I'm better,' Barbara returned briefly. 'What is it?

Who are you?'

There was a touch of her mother's abruptness and arrogance in her manner.

Leonie saw a girl whose pale, drawn face and too-thin young body were a shadow of the beauty which Ruth had described. The bright hair was dulled and lustreless but Leonie saw what

Ruth meant: it sprang low from the lovely forehead and crowned Barbara's head and framed her face as though blown backwards in the wind . . . The dark eyes, so striking a contrast, were sunk in bluish circles.

'My name is Elwood — Leonie Elwood. Hasn't anyone from your home mentioned me to you at all?'

Barbara shook her head. Leonie felt oddly disappointed, almost incredulous. Then commonsense came to her rescue. Martin probably never wrote to his sister at all. Janet certainly would not mention her. And Ruth would deliberately refrain from describing the visitor from London since she wanted Leonie to take Barbara unawares and send back a candid account of the state of things.

'I was driving in your part of the country when I got caught in that heavy snow. Your — mother — let me stay at Felstead till it stopped. We were snowed-up for over a week,' Leonie said.

There was no response, no yielding, in the white mask of the other girl's face.

... She thinks I'm prying. She resents my even knowing where to find her, Leonie thought.

'You're wondering why your family talked about you to me, a stranger. I think the best way is, if I tell you my own story. I haven't spoken of it to a single person on earth since I came home — '

Something in the ringing sincerity of her voice reached Barbara.

'You don't have to tell me anything you don't want to. I am puzzled, I don't mind telling you — my family aren't the talkative kind but they seem to have put you on my track pretty easily and pretty quickly . . .

'And now you say you'll talk to me about your own affairs, though you haven't told anyone else, and you never saw me till this minute . . . It sounds quite mad, to me!'

'I suppose it might, to anybody. We

151

were snowed-up, as I say, and I got to know Ruth very well, and I loved the children. We were real friends. She's worried about you, and so is your mother though your mother — wouldn't talk to me, naturally.'

'I would never have expected Ruth to gossip about *me* either . . . She was the one person I've ever had to confide in — '

'Barbara — it's because you feel like this, that I'm trying to tell you what happened.

'Martin — your brother — and I — we loved each other from the first minute . . . Ruth guessed. That drew us together in a very special way. Your mother was — almost beside herself with anger. And it's all most terribly difficult and complicated and puzzling,' Leonie said wearily. 'But — even though your mother hates the very thought of me, and even though I simply can't see how we can solve all the problems and difficulties — one thing I do know, and so does Martin:

we love each other . . . '

Barbara said, 'Ruth told you why I left home, I suppose?'

'Only that your mother insulted someone who — cared about you, and forbade him the house. Just as she told me never to come back . . . Ruth felt we had the same experience at your mother's hands, that was another reason why she talked freely to me.'

The strained, frozen look in Barbara's haggard young face broke, crumpled. She gave a hard sob.

'Mother may have treated you badly — she would! And I can understand why Ruthie would confide in you. You and Martin falling in love at sight . . . Ruthie loves Robert . . . she loves him so dearly that she doesn't even nag him about being a bit of a weed where Mother's concerned . . . it's no use looking shocked, Miss — Miss Elwood; he *is*, and you must have seen that for yourself. And, Ruthie adores her children . . . I used to feel, sometimes, that that part of the family was the only loving, human element in our miserable house . . .

'Well — you're luckier than I am, let me tell you. Mother sent Paul Damer packing. And I got out just as fast as I could. You know all about my coming here to London and getting a job.

'But whatever difficulties there are for you and Mart — ' said Barbara eyeing her visitor keenly, 'you can be sure of one thing: of *him* . . . If Mart loves you, he'll love you for ever. If by difficulties you mean what I think you do — that you come of very different stock, and that your people may cut you off with a farthing if you marry him — that wouldn't matter to Mart. I once heard him say that when he found a girl he wanted to marry, the one thing he hoped, was, that she'd come to him without a penny . . . I remember how Mother raked him fore and aft for saying that . . . But it was true for him, and it'll always be true.

' . . . I came to London. And all I knew of Paul's whereabouts was the city firm he worked for. So I wrote to him, there, and told him where I was and what I was doing . . . Miss Elwood — '

'It is Leonie, Barbara — '

'Leonie, then; I waited for a whole week. Have you ever known what it meant to watch every post as though you were watching for a — a reprieve from being hanged? I tore downstairs at the Y.W. to see the letter-board before breakfast. It was the first thing I looked for, the minute I got back after work.

'After a week of being in sheer torment, I wrote again. I made myself think that my first letter hadn't ever reached him. He'd been transferred . . . he was ill . . . I nearly went out of my mind —

'Then a card came — a postcard. Telling me to meet him at a restaurant in Soho, for dinner. I rushed out in the lunch hour and bought a new dress . . . new shoes . . . a handbag — '

'Barbara, wait a moment. That reminds me of something. I know quite well that they're worried about it, at Felstead.

'Money — ' said Leonie, colouring and almost stammering. 'What *are* you doing for money, Barbara? You've been ill, you've been out of a job, you've got rent to pay here — '

Barbara's dishevelled golden head went up proudly and stiffly. She looked at Leonie, and with a catch at the throat, Leonie thought, Oh, she *is* like Martin . . .

'I didn't come away without a penny,' Barbara said. 'What do you imagine? Mother doled me out pocket-money from the time I was eight years old, which was more than she did for the boys . . . And when I left school at sixteen, I coaxed her and chivvied her till she made me an allowance. I didn't waste it. Why should I? There was nothing much to waste it on . . . And the boys were very sweet to me — they gave me things. And Ruthie used to make me clothes sometimes.'

'I see. I'm glad,' Leonie murmured.

'Well,' Barbara took up her tale with an air of challenge, 'off I pranced to my rendezvous at the Lemon Tree. Paul was there, waiting for me. That gave me a sort of thrill. I thought, he couldn't wait to see me again.

'I saw from his face in the first minute, that something was wrong. I said, 'What is it, darling?' Just like that and he said, 'For God's sake don't make a scene here, my dear . . . ' It was as if he'd slapped me across the mouth.

'So, we sat at one of the little tables, and he talked in an undertone. And I suppose the waiter brought us things to eat, I don't remember.

' . . . Paul was telling me it had all been a mistake, you see? Oh, he'd fallen in love with me — in his way. But he'd gleaned all kinds of news about Felstead and the Langleys while he was on that holiday.

'He learned that there's quite a lot of money tied up in Felstead. And that I was Mother's favourite child.' Barbara's lip curled bitterly. 'Well — Mother

157

pricked that bubble for Paul. She told him if I married him, I'd not get a penny of the Felstead money.

'I said — Leonie, can you imagine any girl being such a simple idiot? — I said, 'I don't care, Paul. I don't care. Let the wretched money go. She can't stop us once I'm of age, and it only means waiting eighteen months . . . '

'It was he who cared. He was in debt, he was being dunned with bills, he might lose his job if the true state of his affairs came out.

'So, there it was. I remember I walked about for half that night, I don't know where I went.'

'I went to work as usual. But I'd stopped sleeping properly at nights and I couldn't eat, everything choked me.

'I changed from the Y.W. to this place because they began to fuss about my looking so ill. They were very kind, they look after their people, but it was more than I could stand. Then I suppose I picked up a 'flu germ. Plenty of people get 'flu! But I suppose I was

158

pulled-down. Anyway, I couldn't seem to get on my feet again.'

'I'm sorry — I'm so terribly sorry! Leonie said. 'Your family know nothing of this, do they?'

Barbara's white face flamed.

'I'd rather die! Can't you see — the unbearable part is that Mother was *right?*'

'I won't breathe a word of it to anybody, I promise, Barbara. But I'd like to tell you something — though you may not believe me. Your mother is the most unhappy person I have ever met. She craves to be loved, and she doesn't know how to make herself lovable. She never has. The reason she's such a different person with little Rob and Janey, is, that they really do love her and aren't afraid of her. She loved *you.* And she's lost you. She frets about you all the time. I'm sorrier for her than for any of you — '

'You can say that? Even though she'll do everything in her power to separate you and Martin?'

'Yes. In spite of everything.'

'How do you know she's — like you say? What makes you imagine it?'

'I don't imagine it. I know. But I won't tell you how I know, any more than I would tell her what you've been telling me.

'But I do beg you to write to her, Barbara, and just say that you haven't been too well but that you're nearly fit again.'

'Well — I was going to,' Barbara said reluctantly. 'But I can't *take* it if she writes back urging me to come home.'

'She won't, if you write sensibly. It's in your own hands. And perhaps I can help a bit, there. If I write to Ruth, and say I've met you, and that you've had a touch of 'flu but that you're nearly all right, no one can panic, then!'

Barbara studied her. She said, more softly, 'I've hardly taken in what you said about you and Martin. He's the finest person I know. I do hope it all goes well with you both — Leonie.'

Then, with a burst of almost childlike

candour, she exclaimed, 'But you *don't* belong to Felstead! I think you must be frightfully rich! And even that's not what I mean, quite. We're better-off at Felstead than London people would understand.'

Leonie burst out laughing. Then her face grew serious.

'That's partly why your mother is so set against me. She feels I would ruin Martin. I daresay if I were in her place, I should feel the very same.'

She gave a quick, sharp sigh.

'If only people would try to *help*, instead of fighting other people's chance of happiness!

'I will — if I can,' Barbara said.

Leonie's face lit up.

'Oh — you looked so like him when you said that . . . Barbara, do come back and stay with me? Till you're really a bit stronger?'

'No, I won't do that. It's sweet of you to ask me, but I'd rather not, Leonie. We'll see one another again, though, won't we? That is,' she added with a flash of mischief, 'unless you feel you really Can't Know a girl who waits on tables in a café . . . '

'Except that if it's another of the *Carribs* I shan't be able to afford to come and see you there,' Leonie retorted.

'Seriously, though, Barbara — isn't it awfully tiring? Must it be restaurant work?'

'I snatched at the first chance, because I've no training for any work and I should hate an office. And now — believe it or not — I've come to enjoy it! I want to go on and perhaps run a place of my own, some day. Not necessarily in London, though.' Barbara gave a small, involuntary shiver. 'London can be awfully lonely — '

'It won't be lonely any more,' Leonie said.

7

The post had brought two important letters to Felstead.

Ruth took hers up to her room and stood by the window, reading it.

'Dear Ruth,

I went to the house in Fulham and saw Barbara. We had quite a long talk, and I think she feels, as I certainly do, that we are not strangers to one another at all.

Nobody need feel too badly worried about her having been ill, I think. She got run down, she caught some form of 'flu, she couldn't get over it entirely, and the café where she worked could not keep the job open for her indefinitely. By the way — it's a very smart café! There are several of them in different parts of London. Very expensive!

The house where Barbara has a room is quite a nice old place, with a kind landlady and most of the people there are students at London University or the Polytechnics. They looked after Barbara while she had 'flu.

I feel rather deceitful about what I am just going to say: but I believe it will do no good at all if Mrs. Langley gets to know that Barbara and I have made friends. I wanted Barbara to come and stay with me till she finds another job but she wouldn't. I shall try my best to make her come to us for Christmas — but I don't think her mother had better know that either. Barbara still feels bitterly sore towards her mother, and I hope to bring them together again. Now, Barbara didn't let her mother know that she was ill (even though it wasn't serious) because she thought Mrs. Langley might come to town and try to get her home. *I* feel that Mrs. Langley would be equally likely to come up and make things impossible both for Barbara and me if she knew that Barbara were staying at my home over Christmas . . .

Barbara has had a horribly lonely year in London, as everyone does who comes to work there on their own for the first time. This is partly why Barbara didn't throw off her 'flu and its after-effects. She was depressed . . .

Now everything is going to be different. We shall see a lot of one another and do things together in her off-time.

She really enjoys the sort of work she has been doing. She wants to go on until some day she has a café of her own!

You asked how I got on when I came back. It was rather awful at first, but Daddy and Mummie seem to have got over it extraordinarily well. Alaric couldn't have been kinder.

Love — Leonie.

Oh Ruth — she *is* like Martin! I notice it in every tone and every movement, as well as the looks.'

Ruth seized the first chance to show the letter to Martin; in fact, she went across the yard to the great barn, and ran him to earth there.

She watched his face closely as he read it. His look was serious, concentrated, almost frowning.

'Well?' she asked eagerly, impatiently. 'Aren't you *glad*, Martin?'

He drew a long breath. Looked at her, and the colour rose beneath his tanned skin.

'That's not the word, Ruthie . . . This brings — her — nearer than she's been since — the first . . . '

'I've faced that I might lose her, once she got back into her own world. Now — this gives me hope — '

'You'd be blind — daft if it didn't, Martin Langley!'

He laughed, a shaken laugh which somehow sounded young and boyish in

Ruth's ears. It struck her how mature Martin always seemed. She said impulsively, 'Oh, Martin my dear! I hope everything comes out right for you both. I want to see you happy!'

'It's about time there was some happiness here at Felstead,' he said, as though to himself. 'And if that can't be — why then, my girl, we must get out and make it elsewhere, that's all.'

Ruth gave a short gasp.

'I've been thinking that — more than ever since Leonie left — '

Martin nodded.

'Be as patient as you can yet awhile. But one thing's sure: when she came here, she changed everything — and not for me alone.'

'What she says about Barbie — I've been milling it over in my own mind ever since the post came,' Ruth said meditatively. 'Leonie says she's aiming at getting really established in this café business. Martin — that doesn't sound as though Paul Damer were still in the picture, to me. Does it to you?'

'No. Mother would be right glad to know that, if it's so.'

'But she mustn't even know I've had this letter!' Ruth said quickly.

'No, that's true. Well — we can only bide our time and see what comes next.'

When Martin came into the house later in the morning, he got a surprise. The door of the never-used parlour, the fine old drawing-room which belonged to an earlier day, stood ajar.

His mother was sitting before the inlaid *escritoire*, the delicate, ornate writing table where former mistresses of Felstead had written their occasional letters. Sitting with one elbow resting on the table and her cheek propped on one work-worn hand.

The scene dealt Martin a quite disproportionate shock. He had never seen his mother use the pretty, trifling bureau. He had seldom — since his father's death — seen her in this room.

Martin said, 'Mother! whatever are you doing here?'

He expected her to answer with some sharp retort. Instead, taken off guard, she looked round, and her face was crumpled, queerly broken, and the tears were stealing down her lined cheeks.

'Mother — what is it? What's wrong?'

For answer she held out to him a sheet of blue note-paper in Barbara's handwriting. And as he took it, Martin saw that the sliding flap of the writing table was put back and in the well lay a very thin pile of letters in the same handwriting.

. . . So, she crept in here, to this disused room, to read her girl's letters? And kept them in a secret drawer as though they were hidden treasure . . .

. . . And it was such an ordinary letter, after all. Just one more of Bar's duty letters, he said to himself. She was sorry for not writing for nearly a month . . . She'd had a touch of 'flu, nothing on earth to bother about, she was quite well now.

She'd been laid-off from the café while she was feeling seedy so she'd taken the chance to be lazy for a bit! She was going after another job after Christmas. Now that she'd had some experience she hoped to get well and truly into the café business — it was fun, she liked it.

She would write again at Christmas, of course, and what would Robbie and Janey like in their stockings? The people who had the other rooms in Tadworth Street were very nice. She, Barbara, had boasted about the Christmas cooking at Felstead; would Mother send her some parkin and a pudding to flourish at them?

Martin took his time over the letter because he was labouring to see what there was in it to reduce his mother to her rare, difficult tears.

'Well? Nothing to get upset about, that I can see!' he pronounced cheerfully. 'A touch of 'flu is neither here nor there! And Barbie sounds nicely settled — seems to be enjoying her job — '

Janet brushed a hand across her wet eyes. Her wiry, erect frame was oddly slumped, bowed, as she sat. Martin had the strange feeling of something broken . . . or sagging on slackened wires . . .

She said hoarsely, 'She doesn't say one word about coming home for Christmas.'

Martin stared. 'Did you expect her to?'

'I — hoped,' Janet got out on a harsh, croaking sound which ended in a harsh sob.

Martin laid an arm about her bowed shoulders.

'Mum — did you ask her?'

'You know right well it would have been no use if I had. Worse than no use. When Barbie comes home again it'll be because I *didn't* ask her . . . Can't you see she never mentioned being ill till it was all over for fear I'd go off to London and try to bring her home?'

Martin said cautiously, 'Well, at least there's no mention in this letter of that fellow, what was his name? Daker — Damer.'

'There never has been, in any of her

letters. I've wondered and wondered about *him*, till my head was going round — '

'She wouldn't be planning to spend Christmas in her rooming-house or whatever they call 'em, if she were still seeing anything of him.

'That should comfort you?' he added, a trifle grimly.

'Should it?' his mother returned on a sort of wail. 'I saw through him — Barbie doesn't know to this day what passed between him and me when he came here, all swagger and dash and charm ... I told him if Barbara married against my wish, never a penny of your father's money would she see. That finished him! The whole district knows that the Felstead lass is not likely to go empty-handed to a husband ... *he'd* made it his business to be sure of that. He bolted like a rabbit as soon as he knew it was in my hands.'

She got up stiffly, moving like an old woman, and faced her son. 'I did the best I knew, for her. And I was right.

But I wish to God I'd been proved wrong.'

'Mother, don't fret about it. It's over, whichever way.'

'I've lost my girl,' Janet Langley said with a terrible, quiet simplicity. 'If she'd had a grain of — loving — in her heart, for me — or for any of us — she could never have gone as she did.'

Her voice broke. She turned away, slamming the drawer of the writing table so that the fragile, unsteady piece of furniture shook.

'See here, dear,' Martin said, in a tone which he never used to his mother, 'I'll tell you something, but keep it to yourself. After Christmas, I think I'll go down to London for a few days and see for myself just how things are going with Barbie. Maybe I'll be bringing her back with me — who knows? But I'd best take her by surprise.'

Janet pondered the idea for a minute. He saw suspicion, unease, flicker in her ravaged face.

'You might do worse,' she conceded reluctantly.

★   ★   ★

'I must say, Bertie,' said Gladys Elwood to her husband, 'she's very different from what I expected.'

Albert Elwood chuckled. And it was a half-embarrassed, shamefaced chuckle.

'Remember when I said something about sending 'those farming people' a cheque for Leonie's expenses while she was with them? And she burst out laughing?

'Just as well I didn't!'

This conversation took place the night that Barbara arrived at the flat in Embankment Court, during Christmas week. It took place when everyone had gone to bed, including the two speakers.

'I seem,' said the voice of Gladys Elwood into the warm darkness, 'to be learning a lot of new things in a very short time ... makes you feel dizzy ... '

'Maybe we're catching up on our homework, old girl . . . ' Albert said.

It had been a surprising evening.

They had agreed, readily enough, when Leonie said that she wanted Barbara Langley to come to them for Christmas.

'After all,' said Gladys, 'it's the least we can do! Those people took Leo in when she was stranded, and this girl's alone in London, by what Leo says.' She added with a sigh, 'I must admit I hope she's — presentable . . . '

'It won't be for more than a few days,' said Albert encouragingly.

Primed with this seasonable goodwill (and a good deal of apprehension . . .) the Elwood parents had what Gladys afterwards referred to as 'the surprise of their lives' when Leonie threw open the drawing-room door saying.

'Here's Barbara, Mummy — Daddy — ' There was a sparkle of actual mischief in her lovely eyes and a note of demure triumph in her voice. But her father and mother were gazing at the newcomer.

The girl who came into the room was a slender figure in a heavy coat of cloud-grey. Her gold head shone, her dark eyes were alight and smiling, the winter wind had brought a roseleaf glow to her cheeks. A cherry-coloured scarf was knotted round her neck, matching her dress.

She said, 'How do you do? This is very, very kind of you — '

And Albert Elwood heard himself answering, 'It is me who has to say that Miss — Miss Langley. Your people — your mother — probably saved this bad girl of ours from double pneumonia — or worse — '

Barbara laughed, a ripple of delicious amusement.

'Well, the wonder to me, is, that she didn't go down with it *inside* the house! I expect she's told you all about that? I never realised how cold Felstead is till I came away from it.'

It was just by chance that on Barbara's first evening at Embankment Court, three intimate friends of the

Elwood household should drop in.

Mr. Charles Henroyd came back from the City with Albert Elwood. A lumbering mammoth of a man with a head of silver hair like the mane of a silver lion and black eyes as bright as they were a matter of fifty years ago when he and young Bert Elwood started their first London jobs together. He surged into the room and the whole flat seemed to vibrate and sway. Under one arm he carried a wrapped azalea the size of a bush.

'Well, Gladys, m'dear,' he greeted his hostess. 'Come to wish you merry Christmas — and have a nip of that good sherry of Bert's. Going north tomorrow night. Here — ' he thrust the azalea into her arms.

'Charley, how lovely of you! Are you really travelling north in this weather?' Gladys shivered dramatically.

'Nonsense! Train heated like an oven — and it wouldn't be Christmas without the grandchildren,' stated the manager of the London & Northern

Bank, who had been a widower for several years.

Leonie kissed him.

'This flirting with Mummie is all very well — but haven't you got a present for *me*, Uncle Charley?' she demanded impudently.

'You wait till Christmas morning,' her godfather ordered. 'Don't know what they're coming to, Bert — pick your pockets as soon as look at you. Who's this?' He levelled a piercing gaze as the golden girl in the cherry-coloured jersey dress who stood trying not to laugh.

'This is Barbara Langley, darling. And by the way! *She* belongs to your blessed Cumberland, too!'

'Do you, though?' Charles Henroyd said, wringing Barbara's fingers heartily. 'Now, wait a minute — wait a minute . . . Langley — Langley — any kin to the Langleys of Felstead? Over by Carlisle — '

'It's my home,' Barbara said, and her laughing face contracted for a second.

'Might have known it! Remember your father well — anyone does, who ever knew him. Handsomest fellow you ever laid eyes on,' he informed Gladys in a sweeping manner. 'You've a look of him, young lady. Best flock of Herd-wicks that side of the county . . . who runs the place nowadays?'

'My brothers — and my mother — '

'Ah! never knew her. Magnificent old place, Felstead. You can't beat those real old north country homesteads. Can't imitate 'em, either. Glad it hasn't been left to fall to pieces.'

He lowered himself ponderously into one of the silver-and-oyster brocade chairs. 'Tell me, Belinda — '

'Barbara — ' murmured the owner of the name and dissolved into giggles.

'Very well, very well, if you say so! Tell me, if you come from one of the finest old farms in the whole of Cumberland, what are you doing in London?'

'Just what you are,' his goddaughter informed him, and handed him a glass of sherry. 'Working. Doing a job.'

Gladys Elwood's face was a study. And her husband was glancing with keener interest at Barbara, who had curled up on a long stool and shaken her golden head, smiling, at a proffered glass. Leonie suppressed a smile with some difficulty. Dear Mummie! transparent as an aquarium for all her worldly-wise sophistication . . . She's surprised — and impressed — by all this about Felstead. So is Daddy . . .

The front door bell rang.

'I'll go,' Leonie said jumping up.

There was the sound of voices and greetings, and Leonie came back with her arm slipped through the arm of an older woman and with a tall red-headed young man looming behind them.

'Look what I've found!' she proclaimed happily. 'Miss Carradine — and Oliver!'

'We met on the doorstep, or rather in the lift,' Miss Arabella Carradine said. 'Gladys, I've had a devastating day . . . Christmas shopping . . . thank goodness I'm getting down to Thatch-well tonight. But I felt I must come in and see you and recover my wits on the way.'

'Bella, why didn't you let me know you were coming up?' Gladys Elwood kissed the visitor warmly.

'My dear,' said Miss Carradine crisply, 'I knew I should be in a filthy temper, a day in the shops always rouses the worst in me. You would have insisted on giving me lunch — and I should have been horrid company.'

'I don't need any of those excuses for calling,' Oliver Harvey announced. He had one of those faces which are attractive without being good-looking. Fine-drawn, humorous, with irregular features and twinkling eyes and the contrast — for those who had eyes to see it — of strong jaw and sensitive lips.

Barbara looked on, intrigued, amused, a little bit puzzled. Some fresh atmosphere had come into the luxurious room like a breath of fresh air ever since the presence of Mr. Henroyd had surged in, and was increasing with the new arrivals. Everyone was completely at ease, effortless and relaxed.

If there were one woman friend for whom Gladys Elwood had a real affection, it was Arabella Carradine (who said of herself that she sounded like her name sounded straight out of a revival of some faded Victorian play . . .) And no two women could have been in greater contrast. Miss Carradine was a square, energetic figure, clad, town or country, in tweeds and in hats which bore no relation to any current style. She lived in Sussex in a cottage at the gates of her old home, now a school for boys. She had very little money. She was busy from year's end to year's end with her activities in the village, her patch of cottage garden, and her breeding and showing of Siamese cats . . . She was also on the friendliest terms with the school which now occupied her family home, had the boys to tea on Sundays, lent a hand in the San. when there were measles,

182

chickenpox and other ailments.

Oliver Harvey, representing the younger generation, was, in his way, as much a part of the Elwood family circle as Charles Henroyd and Miss Carradine. From the days of Leonie in a push-chair in the park and Oliver tearing about on a red scooter like a Roman charioteer, he had been like the son which Albert and Gladys had lost long ago, and the brother which Leonie had never had.

Barbara found herself drawn into this charmed circle of pleasant, taken-for-granted intimacy at once. She could not have said how.

One spectator watched the unfolding scene, with interest, a tinge of amusement — and something very much deeper than either. Oliver Harvey, who had already heard from Leonie of Barbara's expected visit, but nothing more, came into the room without any particular interest or curiosity. And found himself face to face with beauty incarnate, in a youthful woollen frock and with a tossed aureole of hair as gold and as silken as a small girl's.

But Oliver saw more than a startlingly beautiful girl.

There was something about Barbara which struck him even more than her glowing loveliness. Struck him with the impact of a blow (but a pleasurable blow, if such a thing may be said to exist?) There was a spontaneity, a simplicity, a certain radiant and unselfconscious readiness to meet friendliness halfway, which he found positively magnetic. Oliver had no delusions about the older Elwoods. The schoolboy Oliver had once observed bluntly to his mother, that gentle, invalid lady of great wisdom, that 'it was funny how Leo had turned out as nice as she had, what with her face and her parents' go-getting ideas . . . ' Mrs. Harvey had answered quietly, 'You don't really know Mr. and Mrs. Elwood, dear.'

'Good Lord! Mum, I've known them ever since I can remember!' he'd objected.

'Time has very little to do with

knowing people,' his mother said, smiling at him.

He learned better as he grew up. Which was his reason for being here this evening. There were just a few people in the Elwood's crowded pattern whom they loved, valued, and respected for the simple fact that they were genuine through and through. (His gentle mother was among them.) Incongruous figures, Oliver thought, surveying the scene in his mind as well as with his eyes. A bluff and bludgeoning old financier; who, had been a poor boy when Albert Elwood was a poor boy. An aristocratic elderly spinster who looked like something out of a mordant Joyce Grenfell revue . . . Himself, because they loved and admired his mother . . . (well, who did not?)

Well, there it was. A circle of true friendship and ease.

And into the circle unmistakably, immediately, there had stepped a girl in a cherry-red dress whose simplicity and evident enjoyment of living had no gaucherie but a nymph-like grace . . .

Miss Carradine considered Barbara with the look of pleased approval which she turned on any object of beauty from a painting to a tree in bloom. 'Leo, you should bring Barbara down to Thatchwell when it's spring,' she said. 'The bluebells in the coppice are worth it alone.'

'I certainly will, Miss Carradine — '

'I'd love to come. Thank you!'

'Unless,' Miss Carradine amended, struck by a sudden thought, 'you can't bear cats?'

'But I *like* cats! There's one in the house where I'm rooming, he really belongs to the landlady but he sleeps in my room.'

'Good! That's all right then. I breed 'em — Siamese. Charming creatures, and as much sense and feeling as dogs.'

Oliver noticed the surprise and satisfaction which showed in his hostess's face. He knew her naïve respect for the opinions and pronouncements of Arabella Carradine. If Bella, even

Bella, set the seal of her approval on Leo's little friend . . . Barbara's unconscious score went up one . . .

Old Charles Henroyd was rumbling away.

'Can't imagine why you make such a to-do over Christmas shopping. Not the right spirit! Should enjoy it — '

'Well, I was just making a fuss,' Arabella Carradine admitted with surprising meekness. 'But I've had a hundred and seventeen things to get, my dear man, besides the decorations, not to mention sweets. The gods be praised for Woolworths!'

'Why so many?' Albert enquired.

'My dear man, it's the village Christmas party — the Women's Institute gives it. And then the children do their Christmas play. And we walk through the village with lanterns and the Vicar holds a service — a very short one — in the church, at the Crib. It's traditional at Thatchwell.'

'Oh — we do that kind of thing, at home!' Barbara exclaimed. 'Not the party — but a Christmas play by the schoolchildren. And some of the bigger villages do real plays — I mean, the plays that are done in theatres. My sister-in-law used to be wonderful in them — '

Arabella nodded vigorously.

'That's the stuff! All this writing to the papers about TV being the ruin of everybody today — rubbish, utter rubbish! Come to the real country places, and people are acting and singing just as they did hundreds of years ago?'

'You know,' Leonie said, 'all this makes me realise something. You and I still have our Christmas shopping to do, Barbara!'

'I know! I've kept putting it off, because — ' Barbara hesitated.

'Well, naturally! Who wants to face shopping after 'flu? Besides, it's much more fun to do it together,' Leonie interrupted quickly (and meant it). 'We'll start tomorrow.'

'In that case, what about counting

me in?' Oliver suggested suddenly. 'I need help and advice. What about it, girls? I'll give you lunch — I can't say fairer than that!'

'In that case,' Leonie said, 'I think we accept. Don't you, Barbara?'

Barbara nodded, her dark eyes brimming with amusement, and a heightened glow in her cheeks.

Bye-and-bye there was a general stir and movement of departure. Christmas good wishes — somewhat premature — Charles Henroyd's deep rumble heard offering to drive Arabella to Victoria.

Oliver said, 'I shall be seeing you tomorrow, then.'

It was Leonie who answered gaily, 'Ten o'clock, mind, not a minute later — '

But it was at Barbara that he looked as he spoke . . .

8

'Leonie, there's one thing I think I ought to say — ' Barbara said as they got ready to set out.

'Yes?'

'I can't shop at the places you'd go to as a rule. I couldn't afford them.'

'But my dear girl. *I don't!*' Leonie exclaimed, colouring. 'Not for things like Christmas,' she enlarged somewhat ungrammatically. 'I think it's silly! I often wonder who ever does buy those frightfully expensive things Oliver was talking about. Not me, anyway! We'll poke about and have fun . . . '

Oliver conducted the shopping party away from the crowded shopping-ravines of Oxford Street and Bond Street and Knightsbridge. He drove them along the winter stretch of the Park and parked the car, and they wandered slowly up a steep, winding little street with an old church raising its quiet grey tower at the bottom and at the top a glimpse of trees and roofs of small terraces and squares. The street was lined on either side with very small shops. And no thoroughfare in London has so much intriguing merchandise in so small a space ... Antique shops, windows crammed with ancient jewellery, glass, pottery, handicrafts, book-shops, print-shops, hat-shops, 'boutiques'. And one-old-established haberdashery shop, secure and imperturbable as it had been for close on a century.

'Leonie, do look!' Barbara said, fascinated. 'All these dazzling newer-than-new things on each side, and this window full of woolly vests — and thick *knickers* — why, Georgina, our shepherd's wife who works in the house, wears those still! You see them hanging on the line ... '

'Girls, kindly remember that I'm here,' Oliver reminded them severely. 'We did not come out this morning to discuss these intimate details . . . '

He moved next door. 'I'm going in here. I want a scarf for my mamma! If you can tear yourselves away you might come and help me choose.'

It was Barbara who presently lifted a great shawl scarf in the pale iridescent colours of a milk-opal threaded and fringed with silver, and said simply, 'This is the nicest of them all — I think — '

Oliver looked at her.

'That's strange,' he said. 'You have never seen my mother. But that scarf might have been made for her . . . '

Leonie was on the point of exclaiming, 'Yes! That is quite true!' when she stopped herself. She had the sudden feeling of being outside this. They seemed to be enclosed in some inward and instinctive sympathy or understanding, these two.

It was a queer feeling . . .

Barbara had turned to the pile of silk squares on the counter, with an attractive card announcing 'Half-price in Christmas Sale!'

'I would rather like to send one of these to my mother,' she was saying doubtfully.

And, Leonie realised, it was to Oliver that she was speaking.

'Well, why not? They couldn't be prettier. And they're reasonable, too,' Oliver rejoined with the pleasant candour of someone talking to a friend and without fear of being tactless.

'But my mother never wears pretty things. Never! She says she's a farmer, first, last, and all the time. And that she has no use for what she calls 'fripperies'. She seems to despise them! For herself, I mean — '

'But never for you?'

'Oh, no!' Once more, there was a catch of the breath in Barbara's young voice. 'Not for me. Only for herself!'

'Then, do you know,' Oliver said thoughtfully, 'I can't quite believe it's because she despises them. Or just because she leads a hardworking life. When my father was alive, we used to have holidays in the Scottish islands. And I've heard my mother say, again and again, how splendid it was, the way the women there would work as hard as the men, but when there was some Occasion — with a capital O! — they'd turn out in clothes any woman might be glad to wear!

'Suppose — ' said Oliver tentatively and yet positively, (which is a paradox but in this case a fact,) 'it's because nobody has tried to give your mother something — well, more pretty than useful — for some time? Suppose *you* try?'

'This one?'

'No — this one, don't you think? I like the dark red flowers — '

This time Leonie put in a word, 'The dark red flowers would suit her, Barbie.'

A look of surprise came into Barbara's eyes.

'It's funny — I don't believe I've ever thought about anything suiting Mother . . . '

'Then,' said Oliver, 'you may as well

begin now . . . '

In a shop like something out of Hans Andersen or the Nutcracker Suite, they bought entrancing little wooden toys for Rob and Janey and also for various young friends of Oliver's, who appeared to have a number of such. At least he announced, 'Is no one but me feeling the pangs of hunger? Come along, girls, it's lunch-time, I tell you.'

The restaurant was in another out-of-the-way street dropping like a chine between cliffs from the roar of the Strand to the grey gleam of the river. Every table was full except one, and a stout, middle-aged woman with black hair plaited heavily round her head and a striped apron over a tight black dress bore down up on them and wagged a plump figure more or less in Oliver's face.

'Ah, Mister 'arvee, you com' late! Very late! Two times, three times, already I turn away other persons 'oo wish your table. Queeck, queeck, sit down, before the oyster *potage* is all feenish.'

'Bless you, Sophie. Stop scolding, and feed us, we're starving. How is Patron?'

'Ah, Papa, 'is leg 'urt, because of the cold! But 'e get about, queeck like a crab, always. 'e will be up to see you, presently.'

She bustled off and they seated themselves.

'Oliver, who are they? And where are we, anyway?' Leonie asked, laughing.

'This is Martineau's, my dear. Luckily, a number of other people haven't heard of it, either . . . Best food in London, and, as you can see, no frills . . . Papa and his two daughters run it between them.'

The room was long, narrow, and low, and there was a great open fireplace with a blazing fire and ingle-seats. The tables wore rough starched cloths of snowy whiteness and on each, instead of a vase of disconsolate flowers, there stood a microscopic green shrub in a rough pottery bowl. The warm air was filled with a spicy aromatic scent, because the little plants were cuttings of rosemary.

'It's nice!' Barbara said decidedly. 'I like it! It reminds of eating in a comfy kitchen — you remember ours, Leonie? We always have meals there — '

'I remember,' Leonie said, and suddenly her voice was not quite clear.

The meal was delicious, piping hot, and abundant; that essence of homely, unexotic food, spiced, garnished, and cooked to perfection, which is the art of serving a meal, and one more honoured in the breach than in the observance.

Georges Martineau, a small wizened man about half the size of his monumental daughters, appeared from his underworld in the basement, wearing the long white apron and high white cap in which he had been cooking. He moved from table to table, limping slightly, and exchanging conversation.

He came to Oliver's table, and ducked his high-capped head with dignity at the two girls.

'Everything as you like, *M'sieur,*

Mesdemoiselles?'

They chatted for a minute or two. Oliver enquired about the lame leg — it was a wound from the First World War — and Martineau shrugged philosophically.

'Only in winter, it lets me down, my leg. I stand on them eighteen hours a day, my legs. They are not young, they say, Too much! Too much!'

'You need more help?' Leonie suggested sympathetically.

'We try that. Oh yes, two — three times, we try it. But — ' he shook his head dolorously. And broke suddenly into a rapid flow of French. Leonie and Oliver nodded, and presently he moved on.

'What was all that?' Barbara asked curiously.

'He was explaining that he and his daughters have run this place for twenty-five years by their own standards. And that the girls who gave it a trial didn't fit in — '

Oliver took it up again.

'The old boy has an immense pride of his own, you see? He and his daughters aren't afraid of work, hard work, long hours. And the cleanliness of everything here is a proverb. All they wanted was an extra waitress or two for lunch and dinner, they don't even do after-theatre suppers. But I suppose the place isn't smart enough or — gaudy enough — to appeal.'

Barbara was unusually silent on the drive back.

'Tired?' Oliver asked, as he deposited them at Embankment Court. He scrutinised Barbara's face.

'Not a bit. But — I've been thinking. I wish I could speak French — '

'Barbara, what are you talking about?' Leonie asked, laughing.

'The restaurant,' Barbara said. 'I've been thinking about it all the way back. I *like* that place. I'd like to work there . . . '

She looked suddenly and steadily at Oliver.

'Didn't Leonie tell you that I worked

in a restaurant, till I got ill? In one of the *Cafés Carrib*, it was.'

'Did you?' said Oliver calmly. 'Very smart and all the rage, those cafés. I don't care for 'em myself — but then, as I said, the Martineau place is my cup of tea . . . '

'I rather think it's mine,' Barbara said. 'Do you think it would be any use if I told Monsieur Martineau I'd like to try?' Her eyes began to dance.

. . . And that was how Barbara joined the staff of the Martineau family, at the New Year.

* * *

Leonie had never kept a diary. Her only notion of such a thing was the usually crowded pages of her little leather-covered engagement book.

But from her early 'teens, as she grew to realise more and more that she and the parents who loved her so dearly and cherished her so proudly, could never see eye to eye on many matters, she did, at long intervals, relieve her bewildered young heart by writing down her occasional problems . . . This occurred either when she was under some special sense of stress, or uncertainty, or (rarely), when she was particularly moved by new experience.

In the days after Christmas, she took out the square blue notebook and wrote in it.

'This has been a strange Christmas. Quite different from anything I would have expected. And the strange part is, that it has been happy. Only in a different way.

'It was empty of dates or plans, because, of course, I had expected to be married, and we were going abroad.

'So that was why I was free to go everywhere and do everything with Barbara when she came.

'She is so like Martin that being with her is like being with nobody else. Every now and then her voice is exactly like his, only not deep, it has that slow cadence, I suppose you could call it a drawl, which so many of the north country voices have. I love it! And she looks like him, except for her dark eyes, especially now that she is looking well again and full of life. I never saw two faces with such beautifully clear-cut features, like sculpture.

'But the likeness is more than skin-deep. There is a feeling of something vital and strong and powerful with Martin, and a sort of echo of it in her, young as she is. You would know that either of them were in the room, in a crowd.

'But it disturbs me, too. Because it keeps him before me all the time, and makes me *know* that I can't do without Martin, or if I make up my mind to do without him, I might as well be dead . . .

'And that means problems and trouble which I can't even imagine, and which I simply don't know how to face or cope with.

. . . Christmas was sweet, anyway. It seemed to begin the evening that

Barbara came here. It was quite funny to see how old Mr. Henroyd and Miss Carradine took to her at sight, and how Mummie — and Daddy too, for that matter — sat up and took notice because of it. When those two more or less adopted Barbie in the first ten minutes — you could *see* Mummie and Daddy revising their own ideas as plainly as though you watched them setting and winding a clock!

As for Oliver, he simply fell for her like a load of bricks. Anyone might, of course. But Oliver didn't just fall for her because of her lovely face. I knew that next morning when we all went shopping.

'And this business of Barbie taking on a job, at the Martineau restaurant: I must say it gave me a little bit of a shock. But she and Oliver seem to be perfectly satisfied about it. I know who would not be, if she knew, and that is Mrs. Langley . . .

'Before Christmas Barbie made me go over to Tadworth Street with her, to the party the others were having. It was great fun! There were five of them, the jolly-looking girl who let me in, Jean MacIntosh. Then there were two Czech girls, cousins, and a young Chinese man (medical), and a young Nigerian (London University).

'The party was in the biggest room which the two girls share as a bed-sitting-room. There were trails of ivy and twigs of evergreen everywhere, but done in patterns and garlands, and twinkling balls and little bells and things worked in so that it all looked like a forest in a fairy story. The Chinese student, Mr. Ching, had hung paper lanterns over the lights, wonderful lanterns like fish or dragons or huge flowers. He had made them himself.

'We had the most unbelievable things to eat! Barbie had got a huge parcel from home, with ginger parkin, and a home-made cake, and a cooked chicken and a glazed tongue. The two girls had made dishes and dishes of sweets. Mr. Ching had prepared what was practically a Chinese feast. (The nice landlady, who was the guest of honour), said she hadn't been able to get near the kitchen stove for about three days. I must say she's very good-natured! No wonder they all like her!

'The Nigerian student, whose name I simply couldn't *get*, provided the entertainment. He brought out a small drum shaped like a barrel and an instrument like a guitar. He sang some African songs, and as he laughed while he was singing everyone else could without hurting his feelings.

'Then, suddenly, he took up the guitar and began to sing. No one had guessed that he had a really beautiful tenor till he started to sing western music. He sang *Silent Night*, and *O come All Ye Faithful*, and then we heard some carol singers outside.

'He said to the landlady, 'Shall they come up and we shall all sing?' and she said yes. So she went down and fetched them, three boys, and their eyes fairly popped when they came into the room and saw the oddly assorted company and the lovely decorations.

'Mrs. Manley explained, and the Nigerian man struck a ripple of chords on the guitar-instrument and said, 'Do you know *From Far Away*? Very old Christmas carol — '

'And they nodded, and the biggest one said,

''We have it in choir — '

'So they sang.

From far away we came to you
(The snow on the pane and the
wind on the door!)
To tell of glad tidings brave and
true —
Minstrels and maids, stand out on
the floor —
Stand out on the floor!

'I never heard it before, and I don't think the others knew it either. But even if we all had, we couldn't have sung, just then. Partly because those four voices were so beautiful — the boys' clear, unbroken voices and the other splendid voice — and partly because we were all trying hard not to cry . . .

'Nearly everyone in the room was far away from their home and their own people. And I felt suddenly how far away Martin was, and how far away in more than distance or time was his life and his world and everything to which he belonged. *I* felt a stranger. Because I knew — I know — that that distance has got to be bridged, somehow, sometime. And I felt dreadfully alone . . .

'But after that we all sang *The First Nowell*, and the two Czech girls sang a carol in their own language with the musician picking out rippling notes here and there on his guitar. And then the choir-boys had an enormous supper and we gave them some pennies and they went home shouting 'Merry Christmas'.

'On Christmas Eve there were cards and parcels, and I went out the second

I heard the postman ring the bell. All this week I had been watching every post and simply praying there would be some word from him.

'There wasn't any letter, but among my parcels there was a little packet and the postmark was Carlisle. I left all the rest in the hall and slipped it into the pocket of my dressing-gown and ran back to my room.

'There wasn't a single written word inside. Just a little gold heart, a charm to hang on a bracelet, with a tiny red stone in the centre like a spark of fire.

'I thought my own heart would choke me as I looked at it.

'I got out the chain of the diamond pendant Aunt Ellie gave me and slipped it through the little ring and put it on. Under my jumper. I felt it there, all day.

'In the afternoon I took Barbara walking in the Park and to see Mrs. Harvey and wish her a happy Christmas and take her roses from Mother.

'Well, I knew Oliver would be

walking that boxer puppy of his after lunch . . . and there he was in that long stretch of grass behind the Albert Memorial. And when he saw us, a look came into his nice, funny face that I would never have imagined could be there. And Barbara glowed in a moment — she didn't just colour up, she glowed.

'So we walked back to their flat, and darling Mrs. Harvey was as sweet as she always is. And when we were leaving she drew me down to kiss me, and whispered,

'Thank you again for the roses, my dear — and especially for one rose . . .' and she looked across my shoulder at Barbara who was playing with the puppy on the hearthrug.

★   ★   ★

Early one evening in the first days of the New Year, Mrs. Manley came home from the pictures and noticed a young man standing before her front door.

'Which bell?' she enquired cryptically.

The young man turned, looking bewildered, as well he might. Mrs. Manley considered him with approval. Very tall. Very well set-up (her own phrase). Wearing a loose, heavy greatcoat of some thick tweed. The lamp on the pavement revealed a fine, fair head, and what she was later to describe to a bosom friend as a face 'that ought to have been in pictures if ever I saw one.'

'I beg your pardon?' he said.

'It's a different number of rings for each floor,' she enlarged. 'Who did you wish to see?'

'My sister — Barbara Langley.'

'Ah!' Mrs. Manley drew out the syllable in growing satisfaction. 'You're in luck, then. She has this evening off from her work, you'll find her upstairs. First floor, door right opposite the stairs.'

'Thank you. She's not ill again?' he asked anxiously.

'Bless you, no! Never better. Here,'

Mrs. Manley produced her own front door latch key from a capacious handbag, 'I'll let you in, seeing as I'm here, as you might say.'

Martin strode up the stairs, knocked at the door indicated to him.

'Who is it?' Barbara's voice called.

'Me — Mart,' he said.

There was a gasping cry of joy, and Barbara flew to the door and hurled herself into his arms.

'Mart — Mart — oh, my dear!'

She was burying her face in his shoulder, she was hugging him as Janey might have done.

'Here, here,' he protested gently, 'what does all this mean? I came all this way to see you and you cry all over my new suit — '

Barbara's quivering laughter quenched the brief rush of tears.

'I can't think what got into me!' She peered up at him with sudden anxiety. 'Mother's not ill or anything?'

'She's fine,' Martin said, 'Did you think I'd come to bring you bad news? I shouldn't be here at all, with the lambing just begun, but — '

Mischief sparkled in Barbara's face where the tears still hung.

'I know! Don't tell me! Well, you couldn't have chosen a better time — I'm getting ready to go over to her this very minute . . . She and — ' the bright flush made Barbara's wet face a flower in dew — 'I mean, *she's* arranged a theatre-date, to celebrate my new job, and my boss gave me the evening off — '

'I'm not sure whether I'd do well to go with you,' Martin said heavily. 'Maybe it would be better that you told her I'm here in London, and leave it to her to — '

'Oh, Mart, don't be *gormless*!' Barbara exploded. 'What do you imagine has made Leonie run me to earth — get her people to ask me for Christmas — make a friend of me, as she has? I know all about what happened, she told me the first day we met each other.'

Martin's suddenly sombre face had lightened as she spoke.

'But even if — her thoughts are towards me — there's enough and more than enough to make her afraid. Her folk — '

'True enough,' Barbara cut in, her voice muffled from the cavernous depths of the old-fashioned wardrobe. 'And ours, my lad . . . But the first thing, the only real thing, is to be *sure* of someone . . . And you can be sure of Leonie, Mart. Take that from me.'

She emerged from the cupboard, her bright hair dishevelled from grappling with the clothes hangers.

Martin looked at his young sister penetratingly and in a puzzled way. Barbara not only looked, he thought (with brotherly understatement) prettier than he'd ever seen her, but different. There was an air of assurance about her.

'I hope to God you're right,' said the elder brother fervently and quietly.

'I know I am, *luv*,' said the young

sister buoyantly.

She wrapped the grey coat about her, dived for handbag and gloves.

'Come along, lad. We're late, you'll have to stand us a taxi . . . '

Feeling baffled, but strangely, unspeakably strengthened in hope, Martin allowed himself to be led downstairs. They found a taxi. And as it sped through the darkening streets Martin knew that he was speeding towards his destiny.

9

'This'll be Barbara!' Leonie exclaimed as the bell rang.

'I'll go,' Oliver said, casually but quickly, and was in the hall before Violetta could get there.

Leonie was smiling to herself.

Things were moving fast, when Oliver couldn't even wait to get a sight of Barbie until she was in the room!

'Someone is with her — ' Gladys said, raising her eyebrows. 'Listen — '

Leonie had turned her face towards the door which Oliver had left ajar. So her mother did not see the look of incredulous joy which sprang into her eyes. Nor notice the sudden bracing, tautening of her frame as Leonie's heart leaped, raced, and shook her whole young body.

'Mrs. Elwood,' Barbara said, hurrying into the room, her hand held out, 'I must just explain, please. My brother — Martin — has turned up quite unexpectedly, but he doesn't — '

The young man, later to be described by Gladys to her husband as 'the handsomest young fellow I ever set eyes on . . . ' spoke:

'Mrs. Elwood, you must excuse me for intruding like this. I had — business — in London, and we have all been worried about Barbara's illness this winter. I heard how very kind you have been to her, and I want to convey our thanks to you.'

He turned his eyes to Leonie for the first time. And bent his splendid head in a salute of unassuming natural dignity. Martin Langley, facing the most crucial situation of his life, could not be awkward if he tried.

Leonie took a step forward and gave him her hand.

'I'm so glad to see you again, Martin,' she said simply.

Their eyes met, lingered for no more than an instant.

And in that instant, each read the answer to their heart's question.

There might be breakers ahead. But come what might, nothing could separate these two . . .

Gladys was heard saying, 'I think it's we who should thank you all, Mr. Langley. For taking care of our bad girl when she rushed off to the north at such a mad time of year . . . '

And now Gladys was introducing Oliver. And there was a somewhat confused and emphatic clamour concerning the evening's arrangements.

'There's no question of Barbara not going with you . . . Nor, of course, of my butting-in . . . I only wanted to bring her here, Mrs. Elwood — '

'You must come along with us, Martin,' Oliver said. And said it in such a cheery, taking-for-granted fashion that Leonie's heart warmed to him.

Martin said gratefully, 'Well, if you really think you could get another seat next to any of yours . . . '

'I'll see what I can do,' Oliver said.

'May I use the other telephone, Mrs. Elwood? — the one in Mr. Elwood's dressing-room?'

He came back, and nodded reassuringly at their anxious faces.

'Nothing like a spot of unobtrusive blackmail,' he observed blandly. 'They've lapped up our seats and given us a box.'

The outburst of incredulous pleasure made Martin say in his measured, deliberate manner which carried such rare sincerity, 'You know, I am just realising that I have been a thorough nuisance. I'm very sorry, I am indeed.'

'Nothing of the sort,' Oliver assured him. 'In fact you've given the party what it sorely lacked — balance. Odd numbers are a poor show. Especially — ' he grinned at Leonie, 'when one of them is a damsel whom I first escorted to the theatre when she was six — '

'Oliver, that's an utter lie! — '

'My dear girl, I've not forgotten that ghastly occasion, if you have. My mamma took us both to *Peter Pan* — I

218

was eleven, or thereabouts — and Leonie howled her eyes out when that perishing brat shot Wendy with his bow and arrow — and clapped and squealed and chattered the whole way through . . . Never was so embarrassed in my life.'

'I see your point,' Martin conceded gravely. 'If she wants to talk through the show tonight, she can talk to me . . . '

His eyes met Leonie's. He was smiling. And her heart turned over . . .

The evening was pure magic. But it is doubtful whether two of the balanced party heard much of the show or received more than a vague enchanted impression of the dazzling colours and the haunting song-hits. Martin and Leonie sat in rapt silence. Martin, sitting slightly sideways, his head thrown into relief against the crimson box-curtain where unobtrusively, he could study the luminous profile, the smooth dark head, of the girl beside him. Leonie sat back in her velvet chair, and her eyes were turned to the stage.

But every nerve in her body and every pulse of her spirit was fused with a single sensation: the consciousness of his presence . . .

Barbara, on the contrary, was enjoying every minute of the performance. And making no attempt to conceal it. Why should she? Her clear, delicious laugh mingled with the chorus of laughter which all but stopped the show at several points. She clapped until the palms of her hands stung.

In the first interval she looked up at Oliver, laughter and defiance in her eyes.

'This time it's I who's embarrassed you! I've only just thought of it!'

'What do you mean? Embarrassed me . . . '

'Well,' Barbara pointed out, 'you told us how Leonie behaved . . . She can't have been more carried away at *Peter Pan* than I've been all through the first act! And I haven't the excuse of being six years old!'

Oliver Harvey was groping in his

mind for some elusive quotation which had suddenly flashed to the surface of memory and then, tantalisingly receded. Ah, here it was: *A new experience is a piece of gold dropped in the path. Tread not upon it.*

Tonight was being a new experience for him. He had never before encountered anyone quite so spontaneous, so simply and warmly genuine as Barbara.

He looked beyond her bright head to the tall figure of her brother. Martin was standing now, surveying the great sweep of the crowded rows.

They are alike . . . thought Oliver. Not only in looks — though he's a magnificent-looking chap . . . They're real . . . both of them.

When they came out of the theatre, Oliver secured a taxi. 'Well, get in?' he suggested, patiently. 'We can squabble about who gets dropped first when we are no longer blocking the way — '

'I think,' said Martin's quiet voice, 'we'll find another. If you'll take Barbara back to Tadworth Street?'

Oliver looked at him, quenched a flicker of surprise by assuming a perfectly blank expression, and said, 'Right!' and stepped into the taxi after Barbara.

There was a confusion of good nights and thanks, and Martin called, 'See you tomorrow, Barbie,' as the taxi got under way.

'Let's walk?' Leonie said in a small and somehow breathless voice.

Martin glanced down at her feet. She was wearing evening sandals with high heels.

'In those clumsy clogs?' he asked, smiling.

'Please — Martin?'

'Very well.'

He drew her hand through his arm, and held it fast. And together they passed through the crowds, threaded the churning cars and taxis and went down into the Strand.

The Strand was foaming rapids of crude lights and the inexorable stream of traffic. Trafalgar Square was a sudden oasis which even the lights couldn't cheapen. St. James's Park was a dark, breathing woodland, gemmed with lights. A reach of country night, fringing Piccadilly . . .

Sloane Street, silent, sedate, enfolded in lamplit darkness. And then the homely stretch of the King's Road, stealing into the history-haunted enchantment of Chelsea.

There is something lovable about the King's Road . . . It is like the High Street of a busy, vital country town, with its shops, its market stalls, its Saturday afternoon crowds doing their week-end shopping.

The lights, the darkness, the noise, the movement of London all about them was a titanic orchestra, and their two voices, heard only by one another, were the eternal, the unique *motif* to which the rest was no more than background.

'Love — are you sure, now?'

'Quite, quite sure. Absolutely sure. For ever and ever — '

'Leonie — what are you sure of?'

'But — what a crazy question, dearest! Sure that I love you, of course! What else?'

'My dear heart — my little love — that's what I've lived to know . . . But think. Oh my dear, my dear, think with all your might. Do you care enough to bear what there will be to bear?'

'Martin, haven't we both thought threadbare about it all? Hasn't your mother left nothing unsaid — poor dear — to make each of us, both of us, realise it? We love each other. That's all that matters.'

Martin's incoherent sound was like a smothered groan . . .

'Try to understand what I'm trying to say? For me, the one dread, the one nightmare, has been that you could never come to — love me as I love you. Now — thank God — I haven't that to fear any more. But I am afraid for *you* . . .

'Listen, darling, listen to me and don't try to speak till I've managed to say what's in my mind. First, your parents may feel so strongly that they — cut themselves off from you. That is a terrible thing. I've seen it, more than once. We northern folk are stiff-necked and bitterly hard, sometimes . . . '

'But Daddy and Mummie won't be like that, Martin. I know them — you don't, remember. They'll — they'll get a shock, of course . . . I'm not trying to pretend anything else. But we could never let go of each other — they and I!'

'I hope with all my soul you're right!

'Then — there's my mother . . . I have told her that if I could win you, either my wife would be made welcome or I would make another home for us both.'

'But Felstead *is* your home. You love it, Martin.'

'Yes. It's my home,' he assented tersely. 'But I love you more. And home will be wherever you can be happy, Leonie — '

'It would be heaven — to be just

ourselves,' she said softly and truthfully. 'But we must try — the other way. Oh Martin, I'm so *sorry* for your mother!'

'You can say that? When she — '

'I know! I know! But I'm terribly sorry for her! I — I don't want our happiness to be at the cost of all she has left. I want it to give her back something — not take away — '

It was then, halting on the deserted pavement on the corner of a narrow side-street, that Martin took her in his arms and kissed her as though that kiss could never end . . .

Leonie Elwood; the sheltered, the scrupulously brought-up, the fastidious. Martin Langley; the north countryman who was armoured in the reserve and reticence of his race and his kind. Standing locked in one another's arms on a London street corner . . . deaf and blind to everything but the singing in their beating hearts and the dizzy ecstasy in their star-struck heads . . .

'Darling — your face is wet! Leonie — are you crying?'

'My blessed, beloved idiot — ' her breathless voice shook with giddy laughter, 'it's pouring with rain! And I never even noticed — did you?'

They clung to one another, laughing absurdly.

'Oh, what a gorgeous night!' Leonie said . . . 'How I love rain . . . '

★   ★   ★

'I don't understand!' Gladys Elwood said helplessly, almost piteously. 'I simply don't understand!'

She had come back from a dress-show to find Leonie, the young man, Martin Langley, and her husband, in deep conclave in the study. They had the air of having been there for some time.

And she was met by the announcement that the young man, the handsome farmer from the wilds, wished to marry Leonie. And that Leonie wished to marry him . . .

Gladys stared in blank bewilderment

from face to face. Albert, instead of looking thunderous and purple, was looking slightly dazed, it was true, but quite calm. Martin was looking very serious, and (as poor Gladys caught herself thinking), handsomer than ever ... He had risen to his towering height as she came in, and was still standing.

And Leonie ... Leonie was perched on the arm of her father's big chair, and she was looking perfectly radiant. Nothing less.

Martin said, 'Mrs. Elwood, I know what a shock this is to you. I've been talking to your husband for almost an hour — I wonder whether *you* would care to talk to *me*, a little?'

He smiled at her, very gently, very kindly.

'Could you try to tell me, quite plainly, just what you object to, most, in the idea of my marrying Leonie?'

Gladys sat down suddenly.

She was so taken off guard — and perhaps so shaken by the blade-clean sincerity and candour of this young man — that she spoke the truth, naïvely, gauchely, not with any outburst of anger.

'You have — a farm . . . Leonie *can't* live on a farm!'

She did not see the gleam of amusement which came into her husband's face. She did not even see Leonie's sudden movement of protest.

'I have a farm, yes. But perhaps — not quite what you visualise by the word. It's my home, so I don't think about it, much. But other people do, for some reason . . .

'That chap who writes novels — Simon Wingrove — spent three months in our part of Cumberland, and when his book, *Quest Unending*, came out, he'd described Felstead to the life . . .'

Gladys's jaw sagged. 'That house? I read the book of course, everybody was reading it. They said the book was going to be filmed — but it hasn't been, so far — '

'No,' Martin agreed with a dry smile.

'Because my mother wouldn't let the film company use the place for the sets . . . She was furious with Wingrove for daring to put Felstead in a book. Another chap wanted to photograph it for an article, *Strongholds Of The North* . . . She wouldn't let him across the threshold!'

'Gladys,' Albert Elwood said at this juncture, 'if it's the farm that's worrying you — remember what Charlie Henroyd said?'

Leonie slipped from the arm of the crimson leather chair and knelt beside her mother and put her arms round the sagging figure.

'Mummie — if it were a cottage or a — a barn — I wouldn't care! So long as we were in it together — '

'I have already told Leonie that if she finds herself not happy or comfortable at Felstead, I shall at once get another house, Mrs. Elwood.'

'But I said no! Felstead is his home. It's going to be mine, too.'

'But — Martin — ' Gladys turned to

him, with a sort of pitiful appeal, calling him by name for the first time, 'she's had — everything — always! How are you going to . . . '

'I promise you I can keep my wife,' Martin said, still with that forebearing gentleness.

'And then — ' Gladys tried again, 'I mean — who will she have for company? For friends?'

Leonie burst out laughing and hugged her.

'Mummie darling! All the people I know — all the people I've gone about with — I'd give them all, every single one, for one day with Martin! And I'm fonder of Barbie than any girl I've ever known. And I love his brother's wife — and the children . . .

She looked up into Martin's face, and as her mother saw the answering look which he bent upon her, something stirred in Gladys Elwood's breast, and something rose in her throat, where the triple row of pearls lay beneath her undeniably double chin. Her soft, creased face crumpled. She searched for a hankie . . . and Martin stooped, and kissed the cheek where the tears were slowly trickling.

'I don't know what to think!' she articulated incoherently.

'That's the truth of it! I seem to have lost my bearings — '

'Or found them, maybe?' Albert Elwood said. He heaved himself from his chair and laid a heavy arm about his wife's shoulders.

'I reckon that goes for us both, my dear. We've always wanted the best for Leo. Nothing less would do.

'It could be that she's found it — for herself? Eh?'

'Daddy, you *darling* — '

'This is a time for plain speaking, if ever I saw one,' Albert went on. 'Leo, my little dear, your mother and I have had our own hopes and ambitions for you, and it wouldn't have been natural if we hadn't. But when we got married, we were nobody in particular . . . and we started in a very small way . . . and we were very happy . . . You'll have the dickens of a lot to learn, my girl,' Albert suddenly addressed his daughter, and now he was smiling, he was all but grinning . . . 'If you want to be Martin Langley's wife — and he's prepared to take on a girl who doesn't know how to fry an egg — '

Whatever might have followed was extinguished as his daughter threw herself upon him and squeezed him round the neck.

'I never did like fried eggs, sir,' said Martin . . .

General laughter cleared the air of emotions. And at once a spirited argument started.

'Now, when do you want the wedding?' Gladys asked.

'At once, if you both agree,' Martin said firmly. 'Special licence — day after tomorrow?'

There was a gasp from Gladys. And a sound of vigorous protest from her husband.

'Oh *no*, darling!' Leonie cried. 'No,

Martin. That's impossible! We can't get married until you've told your mother everything ... No, Martin ... no, I mean it. You must go home — and come back for me, later on.'

'Certainly,' Albert said, in what was near to a growl.

'And — and — ' Gladys was stammering and flabbergasted, 'how in the world could everything be arranged, Martin?' A wedding takes *time* — oh dear! aren't men maddening?'

'Mummie dear — ' Leonie said courageously, her cool cheeks flushing. 'There's been one wedding arranged in this family with all the fanfare and publicity imaginable ... and catastrophe and embarrassment and upset, for everybody ... Isn't it only *right*, that we should be married as differently, as quietly, as simply, as possible?'

'The child has something there,' Albert said suddenly and with reluctant approval.

'But we can't have a sort of hole-and-corner affair!' Gladys wailed.

'We simply can't!'

'We owe something to you and Mrs. Elwood, sir,' Martin said, capitulating with a generosity of good grace which was among his most lovable traits.

'I, at any rate, owe you anything you may ever choose to ask of me . . . Only, have mercy! After all,' his smile made his grave, beautiful face the face of a boy, 'she's marrying a farmer! you don't really want me to creak up the aisle of a fashionable London church with mud on my heavy boots?'

So the compromise was finally decided upon. The quietest of weddings, with only the family present. And afterwards, a reception, at the flat.

The hall porter raised a benevolent eye over the edge of his evening paper as Miss Elwood came down in the lift with the tall gentleman who had visited Number Eleven on two successive evenings and the two went out into the night of wind and frosty stars.

' . . . Dear heart, I still can't believe it.'

'I know! Oh Martin, if only you needn't go tomorrow — '

'If only I were carrying you off with me — '

'If only you could! How I hate all the idiotic *business* about just getting married!'

'But your father and mother have been — well, it's a miracle, there's no other word for it.'

'They're angels,' said their daughter, dreamily, bemusedly. 'Darling, I must go in. If I don't, I never shall — '

* * *

Janet Langley faced her son across the table in the upstairs room. She had listened silently, intently, while he gave her news of Barbara. Not a muscle of her listening face betrayed the relief which was so poignant that it amounted to a physical pang.

Martin was concluding, 'You can set your mind at rest about that chap, Damer. Barbie never mentioned him, and there's not a sign of him.

'Besides — ' here he smiled, 'there's a fine, decent fellow, Oliver Harvey by name, who's more than a bit — interested. And Bar seems to like him quite a lot.'

Janet looked at him sharply, and he saw that she was putting aside everything which he had just told her, pigeon-holing it for consideration later, exactly as he had seen her pigeon-hole business papers and letters.

'You saw Leonie Elwood, I make no doubt?'

'I saw her. She and Barbie are good friends. Barbie has stayed at the Elwood's place . . . and it was indirectly through that, that she found this new job.'

'I knew, of course, that Barbara was only part of your reason for rushing to London,' his mother said grimly. 'So, they're friends, are they?' She drummed on the table with sudden, febrile exasperation. 'There seems no end to it.'

'There will be no end to it,' Martin said. 'Mother, Leonie has consented to be my wife. Her parents have taken it — wonderfully. Quite beyond anything I ever expected or could ever have hoped.

'Are you going to be less — generous?'

The dull red streaked Janet's thin cheeks. Then she said, 'It's crazy. The whole thing is crazy. I suppose her folk have never denied her anything, and so they haven't the plain horse-sense to deny her — this?'

'They want her happiness. They love her enough for that . . . Don't you want mine, Mother?'

'Do I want to see you break your life in pieces?' Janet retorted fiercely. 'I was sick at heart to see you lose your head over her — I thought it would mean naught but bitter pain for you, lad. And little as you — or any of you — believe it, I would give my own life to save you and spare you any harm . . . '

'Mart — Mart — she's a rare, sweet

lass, and I don't blame you for losing your heart to her. And you're a man to catch any girl's fancy, be she who she may . . .

'But nothing but disaster can come of such a marriage.'

'Mother — I offered Leonie, and her parents, to give her a home apart from this house. And she refused. For your sake.

'I'm not denying that it won't be easy. It won't be plain sailing. But you've helped me in all else that's to do with Felstead. You can help me in this, the most important thing of my whole life, as no one else can.

'Will you?'

He saw her fingers tighten.

'This house,' said Janet Langley heavily, tonelessly, 'is open to any wife of any son of mine . . . '

10

The Old Church of Chelsea is one of the loveliest of small shrines in all London. And there, in the grey tranquillity of a morning late in February, Martin and Leonie stood before the little altar.

Spring flowers, blossoming spring branches, stood against the grey walls. And the sole congregation consisted of Albert and Gladys Elwood. Oliver stood beside Martin, his best man. Barbara followed Leonie as she walked up the short and narrow aisle on her father's arm.

'Wear white, love — ' had been Martin's only request to his bride.

So Leonie's simple, gleaming gown was white and a close wreath of lily of the valley like a circlet of pearls banded her smooth dark head and she held a great bouquet of them in her hand.

Barbara, in pale yellow looked like spring incarnate, and her arms were full of daffodils.

There was nothing and no one to distract the moods and hearts of the small group of persons. No sea of faces, no display of fantastic hats, no muted whispers nor rustlings. Stillness; and the little church thronged only by the memories of life and love — and death — commemorated within its walls. All three equally the gifts of God . . . The imperishable words sounded in the stillness, rang back from the walls with undisturbed clearness.

' . . . to have and to hold, from this day forward, till death us do part . . . '

'Whom God hath joined together, let no man put asunder . . . '

They turned and looked at one another as they spoke the troth, and the light in their faces was a white radiance of confident joy . . .

It had an effect on the onlookers, that simple ceremony in its simple setting. Gladys Elwood's plump powdered face wore an awed, the almost puzzled look. And instinctively, almost without knowing, she put out a white-gloved hand, and Albert took it in his and gave it a reassuring squeeze.

Across Oliver Harvey's witty, humorous face, a sudden deep seriousness came. He was a little pale. His eyes moved from the couple kneeling before the young clergyman in his white surplice to the spring-gold figure standing behind Leonie. And as though a hand touched her, Barbara lifted her head and met his eyes. That was all.

Then they were back at the flat, in the long room above the river, massed with flowers.

The gathering in the flower-filled room, though numerous enough in all conscience, consisted of friends. Charles Henroyd boomed and boomed. Arabella Carradine had exchanged tweeds and felt hat for garments whose very real magnificence oddly suggested the photographs which illustrate Edwardian memoirs. Mrs. Harvey in her wheel-chair was conveyed in and out of the lift. She had been a very pretty woman and though constant pain and the burden of being almost immobile and considerably helpless had turned her soft hair white and her clear skin to transparent parchment, she was a woman to turn a wheel-chair into a throne, and a throne of merriment . . . Nothing had been able to quench her sparking humour.

There were also present certain operatives from the Elwood Works and City office, including Miss Peterson, Albert's secretary of fifty-two, and the office boy, Derek, with a scarlet begonia in the buttonhole of his smart navy blue suit.

And bye-and-bye, before the February afternoon sank into murk and mist, there was a swift, happy departure. No mysterious slipping away of the bridal pair. Just Leonie suddenly reappearing in warm dress and coat, and goodbyes, and a really unusual amount of kissing for such an occasion . . .

Leonie clung to her father and mother;

'Darlings — *darlings* — I can never thank you properly for the rest of my life!'

Martin stooped to kiss his wife's mother.

Barbara flung a warm arm round Leonie's neck.

'Leo — give Mother my love — ' she whispered.

Martin and his best man gripped hands.

'Come up and see us sometime, Oliver?' Martin said and there was a twinkle in his eyes.

'I've every intention of doing that very thing,' Oliver answered.

And then they were gone. And the waiting car (none other than the station wagon, driven to town by the bridegroom), drove down the Embankment and vanished.

Oliver and Barbara, who had gone down to the front door, turned back into the hall. There was a shimmer of tears on Barbara's dark lashes.

'Oliver — your mother looked very tired, when they were all milling round and saying good-bye. Shall we take her home?'

'Bless you, we will,' said Oliver.

And when they drove away in the roomy, somewhat antiquated car which Oliver kept for the convenience of the invalid, Barbara's armful of shining daffodils lay in Mrs. Harvey's lap.

*   *   *

It could be only the briefest of honeymoons. Arabella Carradine had lent them her Sussex cottage, announcing that she 'owed herself two or three days in town' . . . They came to it in the dusk, and the lamp hanging in the trellised porch shone to them, a beckoning star as they turned in at the great iron gates of the avenue.

Martin put the key into the green door of the lodge. They stood in the little parlour where a wood fire glowed behind a tall fireguard, and sprayed the low walls, the gleaming surface of tables and chairs, with flickering shadows.

'Oh, isn't it perfect!' Leonie exclaimed. 'She said her old Mrs. Crumlin from the village would have everything ready — and she has!'

Everything in the low, warm room and, they were to discover, in the tiny lodge, was at least twice too large for the house. Like all elderly women in displacement, however, uncomplaining, content, and philosophical, Arabella Carradine had collected about her as many of the belongings among which she had lived all her life as her diminished quarters would hold.

The room was full of firelight, warmth, the sheen of polished wood, the sweet smell of hyacinths and dried lavender.

Without a word, Martin turned off the light which he had just turned on. And took his wife into his arms.

They stood, enfolded, lost to everything, before the whispering fire. Suddenly a plaintive voice broke the spell. And a velvet shape of cream and bronze sprang to Martin's shoulder, rubbed a cheek like dark pansy-petals against his jaw, and purred ecstatically.

'Lord! I forgot about the cats!' he ejaculated.

'Mrs. C. looks after them — we don't have to feed them or anything,' Leonie reminded him happily. 'We only have to *enjoy* them, darling . . . '

They had only five days. But they were five days out of this world. They drove through the green Downs, they drove along the white sea-roads above the white cliffs, they had meals at unlikely hours in cottage tea-rooms or ancient village taverns. They came home at dusk to the welcoming and enclosing firelight and lamplight and shut themselves into their own lovers' heaven on earth.

They were not permitted to enjoy it

wholly unshared . . . The Manor House School took the liveliest interest in what they called 'Miss Carrie's Honeymooners'. Martin came in from log-chopping for the fire one afternoon to find the room apparently seething with small, sturdy figures and apple-faces and Leonie making toasted cheese sandwiches in a stack which rose like the Eiffel Tower. (There were, actually, four boys.) They jumped up as Martin towered in the door, the log-basket in his arms.

'Well . . . ' he said mildly. 'What goes on?'

Several shrill young voices answered him at once.

'Please, sir, the Head said we weren't to come near the Lodge or bother anybody —

'But one of Miss Carrie's cats was up a tree and it couldn't get down and it was howling like anything —

'And Mrs. Langley saw us trying to rescue it and came out, and please, sir, she said we could come to tea — '

'I see,' Martin said solemnly. 'I'm delighted to see you. Make yourselves at home . . .'

They proceeded to do so. They also helped to wash up.

'We must be the only people living who had a school and Siamese cats as part of their honeymoon,' Martin observed.

'But you *like* them, darling. You know you do! You're perfectly happy!'

'Perfectly happy,' Martin agreed. And turned her face up to him, and kissed her.

★   ★   ★

When the car stopped before the front gate of Felstead, Martin sat quite still for a moment. He turned to Leonie, her face a white blur in the dimness like a white flower at night, and reached for her hand. It trembled in his.

'Listen to me, my darling,' Martin said. 'You have not one single thing to be afraid of. Many things that won't be — agreeable — I grant you. We both know that. But nothing in the world to fear. You belong to me, now. I will take care of you, Leonie. Trust me?'

'I do,' she answered tremulously and yet resolutely.

He lifted the small hand, pulled off the heavy glove, and held her fingers against his lips.

The front door swung open. Light gushed into the darkness. There was a rush of feet, a clamour of voices. The children hurled themselves on the arrivals, Ruth came running, Robert was swinging up the suitcases.

'Oo — you're back! I thought you was *never* going to come!'

'Uncle Mart, there's a new lamb! You said I could have one for my own self — you did, didn't you? *So* I can give it to Leonie, for her own self, can't I?'

'My dear, it does seem a long time since you were here!' Ruth kissed Leonie's cheek.

'Where is Mother, Ruth?'

'In the kitchen — I think.'

Martin stiffened. Leonie put her arm in his.

'Busy as usual, I expect!' she said bravely. 'Come along — we'll go to her, Martin.'

Janet was sitting by the fire, her spectacles on her nose, a darning basket in her lap. She removed the spectacles and stood up.

'Well — here you are,' she remarked. 'You're looking well, Leonie. I daresay you had some supper on the way? If not, I've a hot-pot on the simmer — '

'We had a bite,' Martin told her, equally casually. 'Come to the fire, dear — you're cramped after that long, cold run.'

'How — how are you, Mrs. Langley?' Leonie attempted.

'I never ail! I've no time for it,' Janet returned briefly. 'You'll be wanting to see your room, I daresay. It's warm!'

She might have been ushering a couple of strangers at an inn . . .

'Come along, then,' Martin said. 'We

could do with a cup of tea, Mother. I'll fetch it — '

'Don't let the children loiter about any longer, Martin. There's been no doing anything with them till you came, and it's long past their bedtime.'

Well, Leonie told herself, it might have been worse . . . I shouldn't have been surprised if she'd met me with a burst of unbraiding . . . or almost anything . . .

But upstairs, there was a welcome diversion. Martin opened the door, without flourish, and Leonie gasped. The big room where she had shuddered over a coal fire was bathed in warmth from an outsize electric radiator. Rugs covered the cord carpet. New curtains drawn closely at the windows, a new bedspread on the vast bed, low, cosy armchairs in bright slip covers, and the walls shining in new paint.

'Martin — you *angel* — '

'Not me — or only partly me. Come here, Ruthie, and face the music, my girl. She made all the covers and what-have-you — and chose the stuff — '

'Leonie, if only I could have asked you what you wanted! I had to guess at your colours, you see? I was sworn not to consult you. I told him it was crazy — only a man would think a secret surprise worth the possibility that you might detest it when you saw it!'

'But I love it! I adore it! Those lovely, soft blues — you couldn't have chosen better.'

The children, half-undressed, rushed in.

'Do you like it? Do you, *truly*? Look, Leonie — there was a bit left over from the curtains, and I *gummed* it on that box . . . to hold hairpins and things.'

'*You did*, Robbie? Thank you very, very much!'

'I made you that mat,' Janey piped proudly. 'Miss Broughton, at school, said what do you want to make, and I said a mat, because Uncle Mart's getting married . . . So she showed me how!'

Leonie subsided onto the edge of the blue bed and gathered the children into her arms.

'If you're pleased, why are you crying?' Janey demanded . . .

★ ★ ★

There was happiness . . . Deep and intense happiness. The miracle, which can come to every human being capable of loving, of every ordinary day shot through with light because the ordinary day is shared with the beloved.

There was the happiness of good companionship and real affection, with Ruth.

There was the adoration of the children and their endearing chatter and their charming ways.

But the brooding, unspoken attitude of Janet Langley seeped through the place like mist from the fells.

She was more silent than her household had ever known her to be.

There was less nagging, less haranguing, less impatience expressed in words. But the hostility in Janet's spirit was as haunting and pervading as a malevolent ghost might have been.

Sometimes, as though the uneasy ghost vanished, Leonie's warmhearted and compassionate patience gave her a glimpse — as on that never-to-be-forgotten occasion — of the woman behind the steel armour.

'Mrs. Langley — Barbie told me to be sure to give you her love. It was the very last thing she said to me at our wedding — '

A quiver went across the dour features. For an instant, naked pain looked from the defenceless eyes.

Spring came to the land. The skies over the fells and valleys were the blue of harebells with sailing white clouds. There were sheets of yellow daffodils. The frightening splendour of the Cumberland fells and dales clothed itself in royal robes of colour and sunlight and was benign.

It is strange, Leonie discovered, how you brace yourself to meet certain things and to deal with them. But what comes, is sometimes quite different . . .

She had given a great deal of honest, innocent thought to what would be required of her at Felstead as Martin's wife. She could help with the housework and the cooking.

She would help Ruth with the children. And that would be a happy thing.

Settled at Felstead, she found that her chief problem was not having enough to do . . .

She took charge of the splendid room which belonged to Martin and herself, but one room, however large and amply furnished, is not an over-taxing chore.

She helped Ruth; but the older children were at school, and playing around the farm till bedtime.

Her tentative offers to do some cooking were tersely dismissed by Janet. And so was nearly every other suggestion which Leonie made.

It dawned on her, gradually, that Janet Langley, far from intending to slave-drive her younger son's wife, was exasperated by any intervention, any intrusion, on her own established routine. She and Georgina had done the indoor work of the rambling old house for years. One small, wiry woman, one large, gaunt woman, had tended Felstead as an acolyte might serve an altar . . .

'It's not *you* she objects to,' Ruth explained to Leonie. 'It would be anybody. Lots of women get that feeling.'

'Well, I'm not shedding any tears over it!' Leonie said gaily. 'I don't *crave* housework! But I thought Mrs. Langley was just — extending her jealous feeling to the house. Not able to bear my touching it!'

Ruth shook her head.

'It's not that, or only a little bit — perhaps. She treated me in the same way and she never objected to Rob marrying me. She just has to keep everything in her own hands and do it her own way.'

Well — there was all the sweeping glory of the countryside to explore. And Leonie had sensibly sold her smart sports car and bought a brand new Mini. She could drive up hill and down dale, and see Buttermere, and Hellvellyn, Derwentwater, Skiddaw.

But — but — when you are a bride of a few weeks, and utterly in love with your husband, you don't want to go sightseeing alone . . .

Perhaps Leonie's most shattering lesson was, that a farmer has next to no time off! And that when he comes to the end of a far-from-perfect day which has started more or less at cockcrow, he is all too ready to go to sleep!

Martin grudged every hour away from Leonie for his own sake. He drove off with her every Sunday . . . And those few heavenly hours compensated Leonie for the rest of the week. But Martin was taking leisure which he could ill afford, gladly encouraged and aided by Robert. And Janet followed each Sunday departure of the little car with a sour, slow gaze . . .

She did not protest. But she never asked 'Where did you go? Did you see this or that?' when they returned, their two faces glowing from spring air and happiness. And once or twice she made some dry, pointed comment in some happening on the farm, and discussed it deliberately with Robert, ignoring Martin, making him an obvious defaulter . . .

She watched them unrelaxingly, ruthlessly. Waiting for the girl to show signs of discontent . . . of resentment. Waiting for the beginning of the end which she had prophesied.

The signs never came. Leonie filled the empty hours valiantly, to the best of her power. Ruth lent her plenty of books; she joined in the eager activities of the Women's Institute and the Drama Club.

She told herself repeatedly that if Martin were a busy doctor, his time

259

wouldn't be his own. If he were in business . . . if he were a solicitor like Oliver Harvey . . . he would be out and away all day.

Martin drove her in to a cinema one night: the picture was one that she had already seen — and he went sound asleep beside her . . .

One spring evening, Leonie came into the house. No one was about.

She did not know what was in her face as she lifted it to the evening sky above the great roofs of the barns and the outbuildings. She did not hear herself draw a long breath which ended in a little laugh, a chime of sheer gladness.

Her mother-in-law's voice said, 'You're looking very pleased with yourself.'

It was drily, tartly said, but not unkindly. Starting round, Leonie caught the hint of a quizzical smile on Janet's face.

'Martin said you were driving over to Calder House. They're imposing on you, with all their W.I. doings and fuss,

Leonie. You're too soft with them.'

Leonie shook her head. She stepped into the house, came up to Janet, and put her hands on the sharp, erect shoulders. 'I wasn't at the Village Hall. You said I look pleased with myself . . . be pleased, too . . . I've been to see Doctor Reddick. Martin and I are going to have a baby in the winter, Mrs. Langley . . . '

Janet looked at her. Searchingly, almost challengingly.

'Are you glad?'

Leonie laughed again.

'What do you *think* I am? I'm so glad I can't keep my feet on the ground!'

'Don't you worry about anything, lass,' said Janet Langley. 'You'll be taken good care of.' She lifted a hand and touched the girl's cheek.

'It'll be right welcome,' she added.

11

Barbara woke early on a Sunday morning in May and lay with her hands behind her head. The events of the past weeks of spring, shifted and glided across her eyes.

She considered them steadily, uncompromisingly, as she had been brought up to consider everything.

She was doing well at the Restaurant Martineau. She was one of the *famille Martineau*, now. Working hard and well, as they did. Everyone liked Barbara.

And then, there was Oliver . . .

It was the eternal Cinderella-story over again, Barbara told herself wryly, and (she hoped) dispassionately. Oliver Harvey, successful junior member of a leading firm of London solicitors, with position, social background, and a host of girls who would be pleased to have his escort. Meeting the young waitress at Martineau's at closing time and taking her home. Taking her out on her 'half-days'.

At first, Barbara told herself staunchly that it could never lead to anything more. Oliver never attempted to make love to her, unlike Paul Damer.

Oliver, Barbara reminded herself, was to all intents and purposes an adoped brother to Leonie. He was therefore in a position to slip easily and pleasantly and naturally into friendliness — just friendliness — with the girl who was now sister to the man Leonie had married.

Yes, but a family friend does not feel it necessary to fetch you from your work two or three nights a week, take you out dancing at week-ends, and above all, take you to have a quiet tea-time on Sundays with an invalid mother to whom he is devoted.

Oliver had become so much woven into the stuff of her daily life, her thoughts, her being, that the idea of doing without him shook her to the core. I can't be hurt again, Barbara thought in panic. I can't bear it. I must get out in time.

Oh, not with any sudden break. Nothing obvious. Simply; don't be free every time Oliver asks you to make a date. Tell him, lightly, laughingly, that there's no earthly need for him to dine two and three times a week at Martineau's, late in the evening, and see you home.

Well, he *wants* to, doesn't he? said a voice.

Yes, Barbara argued with the voice, but he's so used to taking care of his mother that it's given him a sort of — well, an old-fashioned attitude towards other women!

This highly rational argument took place early on a May morning when Oliver was to call for Barbara to drive out to Kew Gardens. As she dressed, she thought, this is the first whole day we shall ever have spent together. It may be the last . . .

Which spartan and heroic prospect had the effect of causing her to drop the powder bowl she was holding, because her hands were suddenly shaking unaccountably.

Barbara felt constraint stiffening her in every nerve. What was even more dismaying, she sensed that Oliver himself was preoccupied and ill at ease.

This is ghastly! thought Barbara. I wish to goodness the day were over instead of just beginning.

They were walking down that long and beautiful stretch of green turf which for a too short time of late spring or early summer is bordered by a solid snowdrift of syringa. The day was warm and sunny. The delicious scent flowed all about them.

They were walking in heavy silence. Some blight, some numbness, had fallen between them.

Suddenly Oliver broke it.

'What's wrong, Barbara?'

She started as though stung.

'Wrong? Nothing, of course. Why do you ask?'

Her voice rose, rang with a brittle, airy note quite unlike Barbara's voice.

'There is something, my dear. Have you had some worrying news from home?'

She shook her head.

'Then,' Oliver heavily, 'it's me, I suppose?'

Barabara's face flamed.

'What do you mean?' she got out in a strangled voice.

'It's pretty obvious, surely? You must know by now what you — mean to me, Barbara. And this is your way of trying to save my face. Trying to show me there's no hope for me — before I make a fool of myself and tell you what you know already — '

'Oliver — but it's *me* — ' Barbara broke out incoherently. 'I mean, I've been telling myself I mustn't let myself — oh good heavens! I can't talk sensibly I thought — I knew — I'm coming to *need* you — too much

— and I mustn't, you see — '

There was nobody within sight, fortunately. But if there had been it would have made no difference.

Barbara was in his arms.

'My blessed sweet, which of us is stark mad? What mustn't you? And why mustn't you? Barbie, I adore you.'

Presently she released herself, glowing, laughing, trembling with incredulous joy.

'Now let's get it clear,' Oliver said, his arms still round her. 'You say you need me, my darling. That is the best, the most precious thing you could ever say to me.'

'I thought — I felt — you could never think of me — like this. And I didn't know how to bear it — '

'But — good heavens!' Oliver protested. 'I've dogged your steps, I've been your shadow, for weeks past — months past. I'd have spoken out, long ago, but — ' he paused. 'Darling — you told me yourself that you'd had an unhappy engagement . . . not so long ago . . . I was afraid to speak too soon . . .

'And then, when I took for granted you must know what I felt — and you still went on treating me as Big Brother and Family Friend — what could I suppose except that you were still — not able to forget that other fellow?'

'Oh, it's not true! What I did feel, was, that you — you couldn't ask someone to marry you — I wash dishes at your favourite restaurant — and there's been enough of — of volcanoes erupting all over the place, because of Leonie marrying a farmer's son,' Barbara said in a final burst of utter incoherence. 'I'm a farmer's daughter!'

'Upon — my — word,' Oliver said slowly with a pause between each syllable, 'If anyone dared to insult me as you've just insulted me, I'd knock him down . . .

'I love you. I want you to marry me, as I've never wanted anything in my life. And you dare — yes, dare — to suggest that I'm a snob and a cad! No, no, sweet, don't cry! Here — this is a clean one — ' he produced a handkerchief.

Later — considerably later — they roused to the fact that a few other persons were gate-crashing Eden, were, in fact, sauntering down the green vista, and that children were scampering over the grass. Laughing in a bemused fashion, they moved on, though hand tight-locked in hand.

* * *

'Martin, is that you? Come in here, a minute.'

Martin, with surprise, went into his mother's room.

'Have any of you — Ruth, Leonie, yourself — had a letter from Bar today?'

'No,' Martin answered, still more surprised.

A smile, an actual smile, of some secret satisfaction crossed Janet's face.

'Read this,' she said, and handed him a letter.

Martin read,

'Dear Mother,

This is to send you some news which makes me very happy. I hope it will make you happy too.

Mart and Leonie will probably have spoken of someone named Oliver Harvey? He was Mart's best man at the wedding and he has known the Elwoods since he was little.

I have seen a very great deal of him ever since the wedding. Now he has asked me to marry him and I am very happy. You will have to get Martin and Leonie to tell you all about Oliver because anything I say would sound daft.

One thing is funny, it really is. I told you I am working at Martineau's and that it's a small restaurant and nothing like as smart as the place I was in before. It is the kind of place we like, up north; no nonsense and nothing bogus, and very, very good cooking. Except for being smaller it reminds me of our kitchen at home. Oliver always went there, and he still does. And he doesn't care two hoots about me being a waitress there and the Martineau's treat me as if I were the third daughter in their family.

Mother, I know you have wondered all this time what happened about Paul. I have been grateful to you for never asking me about him in any of your letters. You were right in whatever you thought about him. I only saw him once after I came to London. He didn't want to see me at all. He was head over ears in debt and he thought he'd got 'a lass wi' a tidy bit o' brass', in me. When you sent him packing, he knew that would never be true.

I never thought I would be telling you all this. Wild horses would not have dragged it out from me. But now, everything is different. It's like dying and being born all over again.

And I am so happy that I want everyone to be happy as well.

So, write and say that you are, Mother?

Love — Bar.

P.S. I know nobody at home has time to think about that bit of garden in front. But will you get a syringa bush and put it in? One of the boys will plant it for you. I've always wanted one.

When he had waded through this epistle, Martin threw back his head and shouted with laughter. And Janet joined in. Her faint, dry laugh, so seldom used, came with difficulty.

'You can be happy,' Martin said roughly. 'Oliver Harvey is as fine a chap as you could wish to meet, Mother. I gave you a hint how things were going, remember?'

'What does he do? Barbie doesn't even say.'

'He is a solicitor, in a good old City firm, and doing well. You needn't worry on that score.'

'What will his family have to say?'

'His family consists of an invalid mother, who loves Barbie already.'

Janet flinched. And Martin saw the contraction of her features, and sat down, facing her.

There was no comfort, no intimate cosiness in the room. For the first time, Martin saw it with different eyes. The vast, lonely bedroom of a woman who had been a widow for half her lifetime, and who toiled early and late, and rigidly, ruthlessly, shut human and feminine comfort out of her life. Not because she had no use for it, as was generally supposed. Because her inward loneliness knew no assuagement . . .

He said, 'Bar has left it to me to fill in the picture. Well, here it is, as well as I can do it.

'Mother, when that Damer fellow let her down, it pretty nearly finished her. She was very much more seriously ill than she ever let anyone know.'

'How do you know all this?' Janet's interruption was a rasping cry. 'You're trying to upset me, God forgive you, Martin. You're making it up — '

'You know right well that I would do no such thing. Leonie found her, as weak as a kitten, out of a job. And Barbie told her everything — They took to one another at sight. Barbara and Leonie were meant to be sisters,' said Martin simply. 'Just as Leo and I were meant to be man and wife.'

'Go on about Barbie,' she directed him hoarsely.

'Well — Leonie took her home for Christmas — Mother — she saved Barbara. It was through Leonie that she came to know Oliver. And, incidentally, to get her present job. The child has her chance to start a new life.'

He waited for an outburst. It never came. Janet gave her difficult, twisted smile. Folded the lettter lingeringly, and put it into the ample pocket of her working overall.

'I'll ask this young man to bring her home, come summer, I reckon,' she said.

* * *

'I know one thing,' Martin said with mild stupefaction, 'nothing will ever surprise me again — after this!'

He made this positive statement leaning over a gate on a celestial summer evening. Under the trees of the lakeside road the farm shooting-brake was parked in shade. Barbara and Ruth were sitting at the edge of the water. The children were (allegedly) fishing. Oliver Harvey and Janet were pacing slowly beside the water, rather apart from the rest, deep in talk.

It was a pleasant summer scene. Ordinary enough. But Martin saw it as the summing-up of a state of things, not as a picture.

'Barbie home again. Mother taking to Oliver as though he belonged here . . . d'you notice that he can manage her as none of us ever have been able to do? He teases her in that dry way of his.'

'It's exactly the way he talks to his own mother. A sort of bland impudence!' Leonie laughed. 'She loves it, you know? And so does your mother. Don't you see, darling? nobody's ever teased her and joked with her — and at her! We all wait for her to play the ogre, almost before she opens her lips. I know! I do it too. One can't help oneself.

'But Oliver — ' Leonie shook her dark head, and gave way to a peal of laughter, 'Oliver just comes stalking in like a crane or a giraffe — one of those long, *leggy* things, anyway — and carries off Barbie, her girl whom nobody was good enough for, and calls her 'Mrs. Langley, m'love' — and succeeds in making her come out for a picnic supper . . . *That's* as surprising as anything.'

'And at this moment,' Martin said, 'they're discussing legal business connected with Felstead . . . Mother told Rob that it was it pity Oliver was as far away as London, old Mr. Stevens was getting past his work, and she wished Oliver were at hand to discuss things with . . . Can you beat it? Mr. Stevens is only about five years older than Mother and the best solicitor this side of Carlisle.'

'Oliver has a human touch,' Leonie said thoughtfully.

'Yes, well! don't go expecting any magic transformation, sweetheart,' Martin warned his wife seriously. 'Mother hasn't changed, deep down, you know. She never will. She'll be sharp-spoken, and quick-tempered, and proud, and stubborn, all her days.'

'I know! She snapped Oliver's head off, only this morning,' Leonie said with amusement. 'That's being human, don't you see?'

'Well, if he wants to feel himself really one of the family, that's one way of making him feel at home,' Martin said, rather grimly.

Wedding plans were presently under discussion.

'There's room and to spare, to put as

many of your London friends as you like,' Janet told Oliver superbly. A gleam of real, feminine zest was in her eyes. 'I'll wager you've never seen a north country wedding? Every woman in the village'll lend a hand. And we'll bake and roast for a week beforehand!'

She cast a glance at her daughter.

'Carlisle Cathedral . . . ' said Janet meditatively and on an enquiring note. 'Would that suit you better, Barbie? Canon Rochester is own cousin to the vicar here . . . maybe he could fix it?'

Her family's astonishment was something palpable as well as plainly visible.

But Barbara's response was still more of an astonishment. She got up, went behind her mother's chair, and put her arms round Janet's neck, resting her cheek against the grizzled dark head.

'Mother dear, we want to ask you to do something even more than that for us. Something much harder . . . Something,' said Barbara, with a shake in her voice, 'I can hardly bear to ask you — '

Oliver said quietly, 'Mrs. Langley,

we've talked about this, of course, Barbara and I. Of course she should be married here, from her own home. Neither of us would have wanted anything else.

'But — my mother must not make the journey. I had a long talk with her doctor before I came up here. It is even possible — I have to face it — that she may not — be with us for very much longer . . .

'Can *you* do this for us? Let Barbara be married in London . . . so that my mother, who loves her very much, may be there?'

The listeners almost held their breath.

'Well, but of course! I'd not be one to stand in the way of anything that could give your mother pleasure in a son's wedding . . . You are a good lad, Oliver. And keep your heart up. Doctors don't know everything.'

Oliver's face grew oddly white. He said, rather thickly,

'Thank — you — '

When the time came, several weeks later, there was a terrific amount of argument as to who was going and who was not.

'Mother, of *course* you're coming down with me. You don't imagine I'm going to get married and you not there?'

But Janet was firm.

'Have sense, child! Leonie must go. You'll be staying with her parents and it's an opportunity for her to have a few days with them.

'If Leonie goes, Ruth must go. She had to miss Martin's and Leonie's wedding, and I say she must go, to keep an eye on Leonie and see to it that she doesn't rush about in London and get over-tired.'

Martin, when he heard, gave his mother a look of puzzled tenderness.

The menfolk were tied to the farm. And Janet would take charge of the children.

* * *

Every wedding is a crossroads for the two people most concerned. But not every wedding becomes a crossroads for an entire family . . .

Leonie and Ruth stayed on for two or three days after Oliver and Barbara had gone to the South of France. The Elwoods not only liked Ruth and found her charming; Albert Elwood was evidently impressed by her as an intelligent young woman.

Both Albert and Gladys were moved beyond any possible words by Leonie's blooming happiness and her glorious well-being.

'Talk about the responsibilities of being married — ' Gladys said. 'She's prettier than ever, she looks about seventeen . . . and she and Ruth never seem to stop laughing!'

'Ruth may laugh,' Albert said indulgently. 'Those two girls are having a little fling here in town, and a good thing too. They deserve it. But make no mistake about Ruth Langley, Gladdie. She's got a head on her shoulders. And *drive* behind it, too.'

One evening, after dinner, Albert Elwood said, 'Ruth, come into my study, will you? There's something I'd like to discuss with you.'

It was a good half-hour before the study door opened, and Ruth came out, looking as Leonie had never seen her look: exultant, incredulous, and above all, fired by some resolve.

She looked at Leonie absently, as though trying to get her into focus. And exclaimed. 'Leo — I'm trying to believe it — '

'Believe what? What's happening?'

'Your father has been talking to me — about Rob. Did you ever mention what Rob feels about — mechanics and how he's a fish out of water where he is?'

'Well, I did. Do you mind?'

'Mind?' Ruth hugged her briefly and suddenly. She looked at her watch. 'They'll all be just about going to bed ... Bettter not pull the house about his ears, at this time of night. I'll telephone first thing in the morning.'

'Ruthie, do you mean — '

'Yes, yes, I do! Oh, my dear, your father wants to see Rob, have a talk with him. Maybe — find a place for him — in the Works . . . '

The house about his ears. Ruth did not exaggerate. The storm which broke loose at Felstead when Robert turned from the telephone to see his mother standing planted squarely at the foot of the stairs, was to be remembered for many a long day.

'What is it?' she shot at him. 'Leonie — is she all right?'

'Yes, quite all right. It was Ruth — '

Robert straightened his lean shoulders. Looked at her straight in the face.

'Elwood wants to see me,' he said simply.

Janet did not demand, 'What for?' There was no need.

'So, this is what comes of it,' she said slowly. 'I said there'd be disaster, but I thought it would be on your brother's head, marrying as he did. I've been fool enough to be thankful things seem to be doing well enough, there. I might have known.

'So, Ruth goes sneaking to Elwood . . . and is all set to drag you off from where you belong, the place you should be proud and thankful to work for. The girl I've tended and nursed, and made free of my home because she was your wife — '

'Be quiet, Mother,' Robert said. He said it low and huskily. But he said it. 'Unless you want to lose us all — as you came near to losing Barbie — be quiet. This is what you've just called it; your home. Never ours. And I never wanted to stay on the farm, and well you know it. This is my chance to get free of it, and by God, I'm taking it. If Elwood finds he doesn't want me — I'll get something else. I'll have my own home — at last — and a job I'm fitted for. And my wife and my children. And peace . . . '

That was only the beginning. All through that memorable day the bitter unbraidings followed Robert as he set about the necessary preparations. Martin was told furiously that it was thanks to his marriage that his family was being broken up. He tried to explain to her that he could work Felstead perfectly adequately, by taking on an extra farm-hand or two.

She was past all reason. Martin offered to drive his brother to Carlisle for a fast train to town, and the last sound that followed them was the slamming of the door as they drove away . . .

★   ★   ★

It was a week later that Leonie and Ruth came into the house. Robert was established in the Elwood Works. A flat had been found in one of the new building estates in the suburbs, on the edge of a stretch of common overgrown with gorse, silver-streaked with white birch-trees, and threaded by bridle-paths. Now Ruth had come back to collect their possessions and the children.

'Leo,' she said as they entered the house, 'you go upstairs, dear. Go to your room and stay there. It's going to be — ghastly — and you mustn't come into it. For the baby's sake, you mustn't be upset.'

'I won't let myself — for the baby's sake. But I must be there, Ruthie.'

'Come along, dear. Ruth's quite right.'

But Leonie shook her head, and squeezed his hand.

'Where is she?' she said. 'Do you suppose — do you think she's gone out — because we were coming? Martin — '

'T'mistress is in parlour,' Georgina's cracked old voice said as she materialised from the kitchen. 'She's been settin' there ever since the children was to bed.

'She didn't touch no tea, neither,' she added.

Janet was sitting at the graceful desk. Sitting with her hands resting idly before her, her wiry, upright frame slack in the high-backed chair like something broken. She turned a face of frozen misery upon them as they came in.

'*Mother* — ' Ruth said. And went to her and for the first time in their years together, put her arms round Robert's mother. And broke into tears.

Janet said, speaking as though her lips and her throat were dry, 'Now then, now then, Ruth — don't make a to-do, my girl.' She looked across Ruth's dropped head to Leonie. 'If I can hold my peace because of the baby, so can you.'

Leonie knelt, a little heavily, a little clumsily, beside them both, and took Janet's hands into her warm clasp.

'Dear,' she said, 'don't look like that. It's all *right* . . . I'm telling you, it's all right . . . '

Janet's laugh was a despairing sound.

'All right? When the ones I've borne and toiled for turn and tell me I've made their home a hell on earth, and they can't wait to get out of it?'

'Mother,' Martin spoke quietly, 'not one of us has ever said such a thing. And whatever's been said — can be forgotten and forgiven. When a body is beside themselves, they say things that have no sense — no meaning . . . You should know that better than most folk!' he ended, and gave his mother a sudden incredible smile . . .

'Mart,' Leonie said, turning her head, 'your mother's shivering. Go into the kitchen and make a good, hot cup of tea for her, please.'

Janet's stiff lips moved in a twisted smile.

'Tea — ' she echoed. 'D'you think tea will cure this?'

'It'll help,' Leonie said sturdily, chafing the cold fingers.

'Mother — ' Ruth said again, lifting her streaming face, 'I'd give anything in the world if it could have come about differently — '

Janet tried to speak, and for a painful instant the words could not come.

'The children — you're taking the children from me — '

'No, no! You'll come to us — you'll come and stay with us — We'll bring them back here for holidays — there'll be *two* homes for you instead of one,' Ruth persisted eagerly.

'That's a brave thing for you to say, Ruth,' Janet said in her ordinary, incisive tone. 'I've been thinking — once you'd all got free, you'd be in no hurry to see me again . . . '

'Do you think we'd forget all you've done for us?' Ruth demanded.

'And do *you* forget you've got my baby and Mart's, coming to you?' Leonie said.

Janet fetched a deep, quivering breath. Rubbed a hand across her eyes. Her own normal dry smile wavered across her ravaged and sunken face.

'Much more of this fuss and crying,

won't do him any manner of good,' she said. 'Get up, child, you'll be getting cramps . . . Ruthie, for goodness' sake, blow your nose . . . Do you want the children to see you looking a fright when you go upstairs?'

12

On an evening of late autumn, the winds swept about the old roofs and walls of Felstead, lashing them like waves of the sea sweeping over rocks.

But indoors, all was peace. In their warm room, Martin and Leonie sat in the soft lamplight, re-reading two long letters. They were laughing, occasionally, as they read.

The big house was empty, except for Martin and Leonie. For the unbelievable had taken place. Janet had been finally persuaded, coaxed, chivvied (her version —) into doing what she had not done in more than thirty years: into travelling to London, to stay, first with Robert and Ruth, then with Oliver and Barbara . . .

The first hurdle was, of course, to induce Janet to believe that Martin, Jim and two excellent farm-hands could manage at Felstead for a fortnight without her.

But it was to Leonie that she confided her last uncertainty. Leonie came upstairs one day, and Janet called her through the open door of her own bedroom. Leonie found her standing in the middle of the room, hands on hips, contemplating the wide bed where every garment she possessed lay in piles.

'Look — ' said Janet with something quite hopeless in the single syllable.

Leonie looked. And then, enquiringly, at the older woman.

'Those are my clothes,' Janet said impatiently. 'All I have. Can you see me going to London in any of them?'

Leonie sat down.

'You're going to your children, Mother Langley. Remember?' She raised impudent eyebrows, laughing. 'Not to Buckingham Palace . . . But, half the fun of going to London is shopping! And you owe yourself a spree if ever anyone did! You've not spent money on yourself for years and years — '

'That's obvious,' Janet said, looking disgustedly at the heaped bed. 'But at my age, it'd be a pretty daft thing to start now.'

'Rubbish! And Ruth and Barbie will adore going with you — 'I only wish I could go with you! But I don't, really! I feel like a lazy cat, these days,' Leonie said, blissfully. 'Sitting about, and pottering about, and sewing for the baby — '

So, here was Janet, in London. And here were Martin and Leonie, with the house to themselves, laughing over the letters which brought them the news from London.

Ruth wrote:

'Now that it is over, and everything went so well, I don't mind telling you that Mother Langley's visit got off to rather a sticky start . . . She came up, of course, prepared to disapprove of everything, and, let's be fair, from her

293

point of view there is plenty to criticise. The size of the flat, for one thing. That anyone could willingly cram themselves and their children (most important of all), into Number 22 Heathlands when they could have the freedom of Felstead, was hard to take.

Then, I think it went against the grain to see Rob looking fitter than he has ever looked since I knew him, and obviously enjoying life. I know this sounds as though I were making her out to be almost inhuman, but you won't misunderstand. According to her lights, Mother Langley offered him the world — And spent her life maintaining it for him. He didn't want it. He, literally, couldn't take it. Now, she has had to see him, happier and better all through than she could ever make him, in conditions which seem to her unbearable . . .

Rob has put on just under a stone in weight since we came to London. Your mother said 'That's what comes of tinned foods and starchy trash out of shops instead of good country cooking' . . . '

'Mother is certainly the ideal visitor,' Martin commented uneasily. 'I rather wonder what happened? I've known Ruthie let fly for much less than that, before now.'

'Ruth doesn't need to let fly, any more, darling. She's done what she set out to do. She's not at bay, as she was here. Go on — '

Martin read on:

'What changed the barometer, was the children themselves. They had been saving all their special discoveries here, to show her, and they dragged her out onto the Common, over to the pond, up to the windmill, down the High Street to Woolworths, etc.

And when she said, one day, 'With all the fine things you have here, I suppose you won't care about

coming to Felstead next summer?'
— You should have seen their faces.
Robbie went white, you know the
way he does? and Janey went
crimson ... They both exploded
'But Mummie said we'll all be going
back for *Christmas* ... ' and Janey
burst into howls.

After that, it was quite different.

Then, I took Mother Langley
down to the school one afternoon.
And the children rushed to her and
shouted to the others 'Here's my
grannie!' as if no one else possessed
such an appendage. And their teacher
asked us in to look at the display of
the children's paintings pinned up on
the wall. Robbie's picture was a big,
crooked house (bright blue) with a
lot of barrel-shaped objects with
black faces and a figure like Mrs.
Noah, (bright red and yellow). He
said proudly 'That's the farm, Gran
... and the Herdwicks ... and that's
you, going out to feed the hens ... '

On the way back Mother said

suddenly, 'I reckon it's to the good, the children having their chance to go to a good school.' Coming to London has justified itself because Robbie has produced an alleged picture of Felstead . . . '

Barbara's letter said:

'I wish to goodness you were here, Leo. Though if you were, you'd be laughing so much that anything might happen.

I thought Mother would disapprove of this house; as I wrote, it's one of those crazy doll's houses in a Mews . . . But the first thing she said, was, 'This takes me back. It's like my mother's cottage, when I was your age.'

The very first night she told me she hadn't a thing fit to be seen, and that we must go shopping. So, next morning, I took her to Oxford Street. Mother looked at the shop windows with her eyes like gimlets and her mouth all screwed up. And every time I pointed out anything I thought she might like, she sniffed.

Oliver met us for very early lunch because he had an appointment. And what do you think Mother said? 'Oliver, I am mortified. When I set out to buy myself some clothes for the first time in dear knows how long, I set out to buy The Best. And this girl's been dragging me past shops with things I wouldn't be seen dead in. She's so used to seeing me looking like I always do that she forgets I could look any different. Well, I don't know that I blame her. I've all but forgotten, myself.'

Then she gave *me* the gimlet look, and wound up, 'You may have seen me looking like the Jumble Stall at the Vicarage sale of work, my girl, but you've never seen me wearing cheap trash . . . '

I started to giggle, and Oliver bellowed. And the upshot of it was, that Oliver said why not have tea with his mother and go into a huddle on the subject and start again next day.

So we did. I don't suppose two people could be more different than Mother and Mrs. Harvey, but the funny thing was, they seemed to change places . . . Mother was almost gentle! (Well, she always is at her best when people are ill —) and it was Mrs. Harvey who was brisk and decided, and pleased to be stage-managing something! She said, laughing, that she didn't do much shopping nowadays and that it was nice to be thinking about clothes again for a change. 'But these two should have told you that I am rather out-of-date, Mrs. Langley, Oliver talks about that Old-Fashioned Mother of Mine . . . ' And Mother said, triumphantly, 'I knew you were the right one to advise me!'

The next day we set out again. We went through the sort of shops which make you feel (me, at least —) that you should talk under your breath like in a Cathedral . . . and before we finished Mother was calling the older salesladies 'my lass' . . . and saying no one could tell her anything about good wool, 'my son has the champion flock in half Cumberland . . . '

Do you know, she bought a *fur coat*? And when she was looking at a dark grey dress, the saleslady, who was extremely dignified and had blue hair, (or nearly —) said 'Madam, just one moment — ' and brought out a red one. And said nothing else, just held it up against Mother in front of the long glass. And it did something to her, that dress, Leonie. You can't imagine . . . And Mother looked at herself, and sort of laughed, and said to me, 'Well — Robbie's just done a crayon drawing of me looking like someone out of the Ark, and all in red. Maybe he was right!' And she bought the dress! She looks about ten years younger since she came. And it's not just because of her new clothes . . . '

* * *

'This is like the first night I came here,' Leonie said. It was after Janet's return, and they were sitting in the kitchen having a late cup of tea.

The winter storms had begun once more. Martin, Jim, and the men were out on the hills getting in the flocks.

Georgina came into the kitchen where Janet and Leonie sat.

'Have a cup, Gina,' Janet bade her. Georgina filled one and sat down at the table. Her long, lined face wore an oddly, uneasy look. She kept glancing about her and her thin nostrils moved.

'What ails you?' Janet said roundly. 'You're surely not fashing yourself about the men? You that have seen these blizzards all your days!'

Georgina's sharp, bent shoulders stirred in the same uneasy fashion.

'Nay, t'chaps'll be a' reet,' she said. 'I'm no feared for them, why s'ud I be? But — I dunno! — I feel put about, tonight. Summat's queer, i' the house.'

Janet frowned at her and looked meaningly in Leonie's direction.

'It's a long while since you had those queer fancies of yours, Gina,' she said curtly. 'I never thought to hear you again.'

'Aye!' Georgina said, over her teacup held in both hands. 'I mind t' last time, well enough. It was summer, then, and a thunderstorm, and the lightning hit the barn — '

Leonie straightened herself.

'What's that? I can hear something — '

'There, now! Look what you've done? Upsetting Mrs. Martin with your daft ways,' Janet said angrily. 'We'd best get to our beds, Leonie.'

But Leonie had gone out into the hall. She gave a sudden cry, and both women ran to her.

The door of the great parlour had flung open as though a rough hand thrust it. A sound of dull roaring, of sharp crackling, swept into the cold silence of the hall. In that single horror-struck instant they could see exactly what had happened.

In the summer, Oliver had been fascinated by the old room and its belongings. He had said, 'You know, it's a crime to let this room *moulder*, Mrs. L! these fine old things are mildewed. And that huge carpet and those long curtains will rot . . . Why don't you put a fire in here, from time to time through the winter?'

Janet had shrugged, muttered. But when the winter drew on, she had done as he advised . . .

The fire had burned all of this winter's day and sunk to a red glow under a dark crust. An old crooked fireguard had always been placed in the wide fireplace. There should have been no risk, no danger, and there was certainly no blame.

But in the wild blizzard, an old tree before the windows had lurched, swayed and crashed, breaking one window into splinters. The wind tearing into the room and roaring down the chimney sent the frail wire guard flat, and a dormant fire, breaking through the crust, had shot a volley of red-hot embers into the carpet. Fanned by the raging gale the flames had leapt up, caught hold. A heavy curtain blowing and filling like a sail, was caught. Tongues of flame and writhing smoke met the horrified eyes of the three women.

'Leonie, come back — ' Janet gripped the girl by her arm. 'Go straight out to the kitchen and stay there — '

Coughing in the smoke, Leonie articulated.

'I'm all right. Do you think I could sit there and know this house was in danger?'

It was a desperate situation for two ageing women and a girl near to her time. There was no possibility of telephoning for help: the lines were down already, as they knew. Not a man was left on the place.

They ran back to the kitchen, and staggered to and fro carrying buckets and basins of water, and Georgina, with a heavy shovel, beat out creeping flames while Janet and Leonie hurled water.

Time had no meaning. Janet had just gasped in a smothered, croaking voice, 'It's under — thank God! we've got it under — ' when the sound of voices, slamming doors and stamping feet reached them.

'They're back — ' Leonie said, and heard, as from a distance, a voice rise in a high, breathless laugh of nerves wrought to snapping-point. And did not even know that it was her own voice.

They heard calls, a thudding of footsteps, and Martin was in the room and the soaked, snow-battered faces of the three men were behind him, staring at the scene.

Martin uttered a wordless cry, and strode to his wife and took her into his arms.

'My God! What happened? What happened?'

Jim, the stalwart old shepherd, elbowed his way past, seized Georgina summarily by the elbows.

'Lass — are tha a' reet?'

'Of course I'm a' reet,' Georgina snapped, rubbing a hand across her smoke-streaked face. 'Didstha save sheep? Ivery last one?'

'Aye, we did thot,' Jim responded.

'Mart — 'Janet said suddenly and sharply, 'carry her upstairs . . . Gina, come with me — '

In the kitchen, one of the men stoked and jerked the range to a red roar of heat, and Gina filled every kettle and pan which it would carry. Martin plunged out again into the driving blizzard and fought his way through to the doctor's house.

Janet, coming and going between the bedroom upstairs, contrived to see to it that the men were driven into the scullery to peel off their sodden and stiff outer clothing and brought down an armful of miscellaneous garments belonging to Martin, and bade Georgina 'set on the hotpot for them . . . '

She met the doctor and Martin at the bedroom door.

'The boy's here,' she informed them briefly. 'All's well with him — he's sound, and safe . . . small, he's a month before his time. Leave the child be — I'll see to him. It's *her* that needs you,' said Janet, and there was a sob in her voice. A sound which made her son, even in that moment, gaze at her in astonishment through his anguish of dread.

* * *

Dr. Mostyn was heard to say, later on, that in all his long lifetime of doctoring in the neighbourhood, he had never seen anything like the transformation in 'old Mrs. Langley' through those grim and anxious days. He was speaking to the Vicar. That good man said, 'But she always has been a tower of strength when there was any kind of sickness. In her own home or anyone else's, here.'

'Yes, yes, I know all that,' the old

doctor said impatiently. 'Mrs. Langley is the type of woman who's in her element in an emergency. But this time, I'm telling you, I hardly recognised her . . . I'm not exaggerating. She was gentle — she was tender,' said Dr. Mostyn gruffly. 'And the night it really was touch and go for that poor girl — I was standing by the bed, taking her pulse . . . and Martin was standing beside me, poor chap, he looked like death himself. I thought Leonie was going. I still think she was at death's door . . .

'Janet was sitting on the other side of the bed. She lifted her head, looked at me, and saw how things were. She dropped against the pillows and laid her arm across Leonie, and sobbed: '*No, my darling — no, my own lass! I'll not let you go . . .*'

'She stayed like that. I saw her lips moving but she didn't say another word. To us — at least. To Leonie — maybe. I'm inclined to believe,' said Dr. Mostyn bluntly, 'to her God . . . You'd know better than I, Vicar . . .

'All I know, is, that the girl's pulse began to strengthen under my finger, and she shifted her head on the pillow, and drew a deep breath . . . Martin went round the bed and raised his mother, and Janet Langley slumped down against him like an empty sack, and fainted . . . First time in her life, that I'll swear to!'

There was peace at Felstead. The peace which only comes into a house when dread and danger have been endured and you can scarcely believe that life, not death, is flowing through the rooms like sunlight.

The Elwoods rang up daily. Ruth and Barbara rang up, and were all for coming north at once, (firmly vetoed by Janet . . .)

'Some folk have money to burn,' Janet commented drily. But when two days passed without a long distance call she grumbled, 'There, you see? Some folk are soon satisfied!'

No one in her family need be afraid

that Janet Langley was sprouting wings
... Simply, the loving, imprisoned
heart that was in her, was breaking free
at last.

Upstairs, Leonie lay floating in
happiness and quietude. Baby Simon
was thriving. And after the first crucial
days her own healthy young system
triumphed and she made a good and
steady recovery.

She and Martin came to realise
something; that however much Janet's
surface ways, manners, and sharpness
of speech remained unchanged, there
was a notable change beneath. Martin
came up to the room early one evening,
looking triumphant, amused, and somewhat baffled, all at once.

'Has Mother said anything to you
about this?'

He laid the Elwood illustrated cata-
louge on the bed.

'Goodness, no! why should she?'
Leonie answered from blissful and
remote depths where such details as
farm machinery had no existence. 'She

talks about nothing but Simon . . . She did say to me yesterday that she was getting Widdowsons to give an estimate for making over the other rooms in this wing — modernising, painting, and so forth. And she mentioned central heating — quite casually.'

Martin ran his fingers through his hair and chuckled.

'She suggests my going to London for the exhibition of agricultural machinery at Earls Court, in January! She wants me to go into a huddle with Mr. Elwood about a combine harvester! For years I've been trying to get her even to consider a harvester. Now, here she is, proposing to take some thousands of her capital and put it into one single-handed. Says we'd hire it out around the countryside . . . and make our original outlay before very long.'

'It all sounds wonderful,' Leonie said lazily, cosily. 'I believe you'll find that your mother is going to leave more and more of Felstead outdoor concerns to you, darling.'

'She says Simon mustn't grow up in a cold house ... And that children should have bright colours round them.'

'I've nothing against that!' But it doesn't seem to have done Robbie and Janey much harm.'

Leonie put out a hand and curled her fingers into his.

'Dearest — don't you understand? Your mother loves those two. But Simon is your son ... '

'And you,' said Martin, lifting the slender hand to his cheek, 'are *her* daughter ... '

And at Christmas it was no longer to be half empty. Robert, Ruth, and the children were coming. And Barbara's absence was not grudged by Janet, rather, it was commended and encouraged. Her stout words to Mrs. Harvey showed signs of coming true; that beloved invalid was better than she had been for years. But — 'You stay where you are, my girl,' wrote Janet. 'Maybe we shall see that sweet lady here at

Felstead, some summer. Till then, I only hope you know your own good luck in having her at all.'

Oliver, reading the letter, whistled softly.

'Mamma seems to have made a hit,' he remarked.

'I know what Mother means,' Barbara said. She knew that Janet saw in Mrs. Harvey a woman who could make herself universally loved as well as giving out love from a warm and generous heart.

The day before Christmas Eve the family arrived from London and the place rang with children's voices and flying, winged feet.

'Oo — Grannie — how *big* it all is here! It's *grown!*' Janey shrieked, dancing from room to room.

She hurled herself at Janet's knees in passing and hugged them.

'I've bin *wanting* you!' she proclaimed reproachfully. 'Haven't you bin wanting *me?*'

Janet touched the tumbled hair softly.

'Yes, I have indeed, my little thing,' she said.

Baby Simon was a source of excitement and satisfaction.

'We do have a lot of babies, don't we?' Robbie observed, peering into the cot. 'Last Christmas it was Martie, and now it's this!'

After the prolonged and hilarious business of getting all the small, smaller, and smallest fry bathed and put away for the night, the family came down from various quarters of the house and gathered in the kitchen and subsided thankfully into the high, rush-bottomed chairs.

'I hardly know where to begin!' Ruth said, laughing. 'Mother, I feel as if it were years since we were here!'

Janet's face showed a swift flicker of gratification.

'Well, since we are all here at last, there's something I've had in mind to tell you. And now is as good a time as any, I reckon. It concerns you all, because there'll be money-matters to adjust.

'I'm thinking maybe I'll move out — '

'Move where?' Martin asked sharply.

'To one of those cottages I heard so much about a while back,' she retorted with her usual dry smile. 'I'm planning to have a considerable amount done to this place, as Leonie knows. If you all feel that Felstead is a handy sort of place to come back to now and then and bring the children for holidays — then I think it could do with some changes. Central heating . . . a lick of paint indoors — maybe the little sewing-room would make another bathroom — '

Her family gazed at her, wide-eyed and all but open-mouthed. Janet's face was expressionless and her tone without special emphasis. But it was to be seen that she was enjoying herself . . .

'I'm not so young as I was, and I could do with a bit of a rest. I'm minded to leave Felstead to you young folk, and move into something smaller myself.'

There was a moment of stunned

silence. Then Leonie burst out laughing . . .

She left her chair and knelt by Janet in her usual characteristic fashion and covered Janet's hands with her own.

'And you really think Mart and I would rattle round here by ourselves like peas in a barrel, with you in a cottage? If I believed one word about your wanting a rest, where should you rest but in your own home with us to look after you?

'But it's the very first untruth I've ever heard you tell, Mother Langley! I'm ashamed of you!'

She hugged Janet.

'If you go, we go,' Martin said cheerfully. 'And then what happens to your brand-new machinery and your hot pipes and your film-star new bathroom?'

He gave a roar of deep laughter.

'Try again?' he suggested. 'think up something better to tell us?'

Robert cleared his throat.

'Mother — is it the machinery you

can't bear to think of? If so — we'd sooner see Felstead stay as it is than think of it without you — '

Janet was laughing now, laughing till her keen eyes were watering.

'Lad — it'd take more than some bits of machinery to drive me out of the place!' she got out.

'How *can* you think of doing such a thing to the children?' Ruth demanded. 'What do you imagine Robbie and Janey would say? Ever since you were with us in October, it's been nothing but 'When are we going to Gran?' Not to Felstead. To *you*.'

Janet said slowly, 'There have been times in plenty when you'd have been glad to have Felstead to yourselves — I've known that. Well — you're all married — happily married — and on your own, now. I got thinking — '

'That's your mistake,' Martin interrupted firmly, and the twinkle was in his eyes though he was keeping a straight face. 'Don't think, Mrs. Langley. Leave that to the other Mrs. Langleys.'

Leonie yawned like a kitten, stretched. 'Pull me up, Martin. What about us all going to bed? Tomorrow's going to be quite a day. The children have already said that Daddie and Uncle Mart are going down to Spruce Hollow to cut evergreens 'to go all over the house'. And there's the tree to decorate.'

'We'll have a cup of tea first,' Janet decreed.

Robert crossed the room and switched on the wireless. The woven voices of carol-singers poured into the room.

'*From far away we came to you*
The snow on the pane and the
wind on the door,
To tell of glad tidings plain and
true.
Minstrels and maids, stand out on
the floor,
Stand out on the floor . . . '

They listened, moving quietly between dresser and table. Ruth paused, her hand on the tap. Leonie set cups and saucers soundlessly.

The spell lay upon them, without their even recognising it. *From far away* ... just so had the supreme bestowal of Love Eternal come to the world on a winter's night centuries ago. Just so had love and joy and new understanding come to this house of shadows when a girl, blown like a lost sea-gull on the winter blast, was sheltered within these walls.

THE END

Other titles in the
Linford Romance Library:

DARK SUSPICION

Susan Udy

When Aunt Jessica asks Caitlin to help run her art gallery while she is in hospital, Caitlin agrees. She hadn't bargained on having to deal with a series of thefts, however — or Jessica's insistence that Caitlin's new employer, Nicholas Millward, must be responsible. Nicholas is as ruthless as he is handsome, but would he really stoop to theft? And what can Caitlin do when she finds herself in the grip of a passion too powerful to resist?

HER SEARCHING HEART

Phyllis Mallet

A proposal of marriage from Robert, whom she does not love, brings Valerie face to face with a frightening question — is she incapable of falling in love? She rejects Robert and flees to the tranquility of Cornwall, hoping to find the answer; but when she meets Bruce and his motherless young daughter Mandy, she discovers new and disturbing emotions deep in her heart — and finds the answer to her question . . .